IT'S ME

OR HER

BOOKS BY VICTORIA JENKINS

The Divorce

The Argument

The Accusation

The Playdate

The New Family

The Bridesmaids

The Midwife

Happily Married

Your Perfect Life

The Open Marriage

The Mother's Phone Call

The Woman in Our Marriage

DETECTIVES KING AND LANE SERIES

The Girls in the Water

The First One to Die

Nobody's Child

A Promise to the Dead

VICTORIA JENKINS

IT'S ME

OR

HER

bookouture

Published by Bookouture in 2025

An imprint of Storyfire Ltd.
Carmelite House
50 Victoria Embankment
London EC4Y 0DZ

www.bookouture.com

The authorised representative in the EEA is Hachette Ireland
8 Castlecourt Centre
Dublin 15 D15 XTP3
Ireland
(email: info@hbgi.ie)

Copyright © Victoria Jenkins, 2025

Victoria Jenkins has asserted her right to be identified
as the author of this work.

All rights reserved. No part of this publication may be reproduced, stored in any retrieval system, or transmitted, in any form or by any means, electronic, mechanical, photocopying, recording or otherwise, without the prior written permission of the publishers.

ISBN: 978-1-80550-357-6
eBook ISBN: 978-1-80550-356-9

This book is a work of fiction. Names, characters, businesses, organizations, places and events other than those clearly in the public domain, are either the product of the author's imagination or are used fictitiously. Any resemblance to actual persons, living or dead, events or locales is entirely coincidental.

PROLOGUE

There are two things needed to start a fire: heat and fuel. At one point, we had both those things in abundance, and the spark between us had burned with an intensity that could scorch through anything that stood in our way. Together, we were a fireball that could destroy anyone who crossed our path.

Now, I stand and watch as the flames catch quickly. A single spark, that was all it took. Not all that different from falling in love at first sight, really. First there's a heat that builds quickly, deceptively warming before it begins to burn. Then come the flames that rise high, blinding a person to anything else. Eventually, the fire dies out, and everything it has touched is left ruined.

Beyond the door, I hear something. A sound beneath the roar of the fire, muffled and uncertain. But when you've been as burned as I have, you learn to shut things out. Lies. Betrayal. Pleas. I remind myself that this isn't my fault... that this is only what I've been driven to. This is what they made me do.

This house was already a shell, long before the fire was started. A castle built on sand... a house of cards that turned out to be a pack filled with jokers. But I was the fool for believing it might have ever been anything different.

Betrayal is a strange thing. It doesn't come all at once, making its arrival known at the door like an uninvited guest. It breaks into your home, invisible and insidious, like a thief in the night that edges its way in slowly. By the time you realise it's with you, it's too late, and there is nothing left to salvage. Destruction never announces itself – it simply takes, reducing everything to ash before you can beg for it back. But I will never be seen begging. And so, I let it burn. I stand back as the flames rise upwards, and I watch as my life is consumed by the fire.

ONE

I slip an emerald-green Christmas jumper with a sequinned robin design back on to its hanger and push it against the others on the rack. It's still October, but Christmas is already everywhere, the department store decorated with elaborate garlands that hang from the ceilings and ornate Christmas trees that flank the foot of every escalator. Two storeys down, the entire basement floor has been transformed into a winter wonderland, with faux fireplaces and display doorways selling an aspirational festive aesthetic most people can't dream of ever being able to afford.

And I certainly can't, not on what I earn.

'Excuse me.'

I turn to find a man standing just behind me, a perfume tester bottle held in each hand. The first thing I notice about him is the stubble that shades his jawline, just enough to keep him from looking too polished, and when my eyes meet his, having first travelled the contours of his Hugo Boss-campaign face, I'm met with a smile that manages to settle way beyond the deep brown of his irises.

'Can I help you?' I say, and my voice catches midway

through the words, making them sound as though they've been strangled. *Daisy, you idiot.* I feel a flush begin to rise in my chest, and the more I try to ignore it, the hotter I feel myself becoming. I've never reacted to a man this way, and it makes me feel weirdly exposed, as though he's caught me standing here naked.

'I just need a second opinion,' he tells me. 'If you don't mind?' He holds the tester bottles up in front of him. 'Which one would you go for? It's for my mother's birthday. I haven't got a clue what I'm doing.'

I glance at the names on the bottles. I don't know a thing about perfume; I've worn the same, trusted affordable scent since my late teens, only veering from it when I've been able to use my staff discount on top of a sale price.

'I suppose it depends what type of woman your mother is,' I say, reaching for the bottle in his right hand. 'May I?' He passes it to me, and our fingertips brush slightly. I swear I've just been jolted with a bolt of electricity that races straight up my arm and lands in places it shouldn't.

I spray the scent into the air between us, praying he can't somehow read my thoughts. I should probably have called Lorna over; she'll know more about perfume than I do. I would have been spared the awkwardness of having to stand here blushing like a schoolgirl with a crush on her hot teacher.

'This one's a bit spicy,' I say, handing him back the bottle.

'Spicy,' he repeats, maintaining eye contact. 'Okay.'

Is he flirting with me? With just two words, he's managed to send a flame of heat up the back of my neck, creeping now perilously close to my face, and he's looking at me like he knows what I'm thinking. And I'm sure he knows exactly what he's doing.

I take the other bottle from him. 'This one's more floral. More subtle. Which do you think your mother would prefer?'

He takes the second bottle from me and studies both the

labels. 'It would be a bit strange if I chose the spicy one for my mother, wouldn't it?' he says, with a playful smile. 'So I guess I'll go for this one. Thanks for your help,' and his eyes fall to the name badge on my chest. 'Daisy. Floral.' He raises the chosen tester bottle. 'It was meant to be.'

The flush lands squarely on my cheeks, and I silently berate myself for reacting this way to a stranger. How old is this man? Late-thirties? A few years older than I am. He's good-looking in the kind of way I suppose a lot of men must be – tall, dark-eyed, brooding – yet I can't remember ever being attracted to a face the way I am to his.

Get a grip of yourself, for goodness' sake.

'Shall I get you the boxed one?' I offer, desperate to break the silence that has settled between us. 'We've got it in fifty or one hundred mils.'

'I'll have the one hundred, please. She only gets one birthday a year, after all.'

I take both the testers from him. My hands are clammy, and for an uncomfortable moment I'm worried that my sweaty fingers might have grazed his. He waits by the rack of Christmas jumpers when I go to get the box of perfume, and as I turn the corner, Aisha calls me over to the customer service desk.

'Who's the bloke?' she asks.

'What bloke?'

Her right eyebrow rises to an arch. 'The one practically salivating over you.' She steps from behind the desk. 'And buying you perfume already.' She laughs as I glance over my shoulder to check he's not within earshot.

'You know Lorna was right over by those when he picked them up,' she tells me, following me to collect the box from behind the perfume counter. 'He could have easily asked her for help.'

'Stop it,' I say teasingly as she shoots me a look.

'What? I'm just saying.'

She scoots off when she notices the department manager speaking to another member of staff close by, and when I return to the rack of Christmas jumpers, the man with the mother is standing looking at his phone. I realise this is how I'll think of him after he's left – the man with the mother. Then it strikes me as odd that I might think of him at all. I can't remember a time I've ever given a customer a second thought once they've walked away.

'You're a star,' he says, taking the bottle from me. 'Thank you, Daisy.'

He maintains eye contact as he speaks my name, the word falling from his lips like a whisper.

'I can gift wrap it for you, if you like.'

Oh my God... my voice sounds nothing like my own.

'That would be perfect.'

He's still looking at me with that intense and prolonged eye contact. His lips close and part on the 'p' of perfect, puckering like a kiss.

'This way,' I say, distracted by the inappropriateness of my thoughts.

I scan the item, and he taps his card against the reader, watching as I set about wrapping the perfume in sparkly gold paper.

'She'll ask me who I got to choose that,' he says, as I tie a ribbon around the box and knot it with a bow. 'And wrap it. She'll know it wasn't me. You know what mothers are like.'

I smile politely. I don't know what they're like. My mother died when I was five years old. I have a memory of her in the garden, one arm wrapped around me, the other around my brother as the three of us posed for a picture, my dad behind the camera. And then another: me at the side of a bed that didn't belong to our house, my mother thin-limbed and sad-eyed beneath a blanket that wasn't hers, smiling despite the pain. Other than this, I can barely remember her in any detail other than those that have been offered by the few photographs that remain.

'Thanks for your help, Daisy,' he says, as I hand him his mother's present in a paper bag. 'It was nice to meet you.'

I'm sure he waits a moment longer than is necessary to take the bag from my hand.

'You're welcome.' *It was nice to meet you too*, I think, but I don't say it. Because I know I'm unlikely to see this man again, and the fact shouldn't bother me. Yet the idea of never seeing him again leaves me feeling strangely empty as I watch him walk away.

TWO

I work longer shifts than the average so that I can afford to take three days a week off work rather than two. It seemed to make sense when I'd proposed the idea to my boss, a healthy work/life balance, and as I hate the commute from Pontypridd to Cardiff, it reduces the days I need to do it. Though there are some days when I wonder what I'm going to do with the time when I'm not at work. When they offer extra hours, I often take them. And if anyone's ever sick, I'm always the first person to be contacted for cover. The extra money always helps. But it's not just that. Sometimes, I'd rather be at the store. The noise and the busyness of the place makes the hours pass quickly, and there's always someone to talk to, whether customers or other staff. The flat can get a bit too quiet sometimes.

I go to see Aisha before I clock off for the end of my shift, finding her in the middle of processing an online return for a woman complaining about the inaccurate sizing of a gilet. I wait and listen as the lady laments clothing not being made like it used to be, and once she's completed the refund and apologised for what must be the fourth time, Aisha gestures to the female toilets, where we hide for the next five minutes and discuss our plans for the weekend.

'Do you fancy the comedy club tomorrow?' she suggests, running a fingertip beneath her left eye to wipe away a smudge of mascara. Aisha is blessed with the longest natural eyelashes I've ever seen, but it means that whenever her eyes water, whether through laughter or yawns – I've never once seen her cry – she's left with little black spiders on her eyelids.

'How much are the tickets?'

'Not sure. I'll check later and text you. You're still sure you don't fancy a repeat of the last one?'

Once a month, every month, Aisha and I have a night out together, sometimes trying something new, but usually ending up in one of the city's nightclubs. We've conceded that now, both in our thirties, we're getting a bit too old to be dancing until the early hours of the following morning, but Aisha's not going to give in to societal expectations without an alcohol-free fight, and I admire her tenacity in the face of time's inevitability. Watching the struggles her ageing grandparents are going through seems to have given her a 'seize the moment' attitude.

She's never drunk alcohol, but five hours of dancing in high-heeled shoes can have similar effects on the body as a two-day hangover, and after last month's night out, we'd vowed to try something that involved at least intermittent periods of sitting down.

'We could always do a takeaway at mine,' I suggest, meeting her eye in the mirror and smiling.

Her hand falls from her face as she turns to me. 'And a game of Scrabble for dessert? The nursing home's not calling just yet, Miss White.'

'You've heard the rumours about those places though?'

'What rumours?'

'Orgy dens for the retired.'

Aisha snort-laughs. 'Thanks for the unwanted mental image.'

'You're welcome. I'll look at the comedy club website later and let you know.'

She slips back to her department after we leave the toilets, and I go to the staff room to get my coat and bag. Once I've got my phone, the first thing I do is check my emails. I went to an interview last week for another job: a supervisor's position at a supermarket chain. I didn't tell Aisha. She'll be disappointed that I'm planning to leave, and there didn't seem any point in mentioning it before I'd even been to an interview. After a week of waiting, I'd written off the idea of getting a response from them, assuming I'd been unsuccessful. But when I check my inbox, there's an email.

I scan the content before landing on the important sentence.

We regret to inform you that on this occasion...

I delete the rejection. A part of me is relieved: I love it here, despite it probably now being my comfort zone. The problem is that opportunities for promotion rarely arise, and I can't stay on what I'm currently earning for the rest of my life. In an ideal world, I would stay where I am, but I know enough of life to know that ideal is a rarity most people aren't lucky enough to stumble upon.

I've never had a desire for expensive clothes or a big house. I just want to be comfortable, which doesn't feel too lavish a dream.

I slip my phone into my coat pocket and try to shake off the disappointment. Self-pity never helped change anything.

I make my way to the staff doors at the back of the building, where the deliveries are made. There's a square loading area fenced with high metal railings, then a path that runs around the store and links with a lane at the back of the neighbouring shops and restaurants. It's a shortcut to the train station at the other end of Cardiff's main shopping street, so I always cut through here.

It's colder tonight than it's been since last winter, and as I zip my coat up closer to my chin, I shove my other shoulder up to straighten the bag I'm carrying. That's when I hear it. A noise just behind me, like something being shifted. Like someone moving.

I turn sharply, and everything that follows happens so quickly. A young man lunges at me, appearing from out of the shadows. I'm guessing he's young because of his narrow frame and the agility of his movements, though in the darkness and with his hood pulled up, I can't see his face at all. I cry out as he grabs me by the arm, and when I try to fight him off, he shoves me in the chest, flinging me across the lane like a bag of rubbish. I stumble and fall forwards, and a searing pain tears through my cheek as my face hits something cold and sharp before I hit the ground.

He's already fleeing, taking my handbag with him. I don't bother to chase after him; for all I know, he could be carrying a knife. I think of my phone and my keys in the bag – so much of my life disappearing into the darkness. Then I pat down my pockets, remembering the email I read not long ago. My phone is still there. It's something, at least. I put my fingers to my face as I hurry along, hobbling out of the lane on an ankle that feels twisted. Beneath a streetlight, I study my hand. My fingertips are stained bright red with blood. I pull my coat hood up and try to shield my injured face as I shakily make my way to the train station.

THREE

The train is never usually this busy. The only seat unoccupied has got someone's shopping piled on it, and when I stop and silently gesture to it, the owner in question huffs unapologetically and pulls her bags on to her lap, disgruntled at having to share a public space. She takes a second glance at my face as I sit, her lip curling with judgement. I wonder just how bad I look; I've not yet managed to catch a glimpse of my reflection in a shop window.

I move for the woman beside me to get off at the next stop, and once she's gone, I settle into the window seat. Now, for the first time, I see the state of myself. Faded to grey in the darkened reflection of the train window, the injury to my face is a two-inch split that's splattered blood across my nose and on my top lip. I must have caught my face on the latch of one of the gates when I fell. No wonder I've been on the receiving end of some wary glances.

Concrete block buildings turn to a blur of hedgerows and terraces as we move further from the city, first past the student area and then through the suburbs. Lit kitchen windows show couples and families gathered together, and my heart tightens at the promise of my empty flat.

I close my eyes and lean back into the headrest, trying to shut myself off from the world, when I hear someone speak to me.

'Hello again.'

My eyes snap open at the sound of his voice. It's him and he's standing in the aisle, holding the brown paper bag I gave him just a few hours ago.

'What's happened to your face?' he asks, his voice laced with genuine concern.

'Oh, it was nothing,' I tell him, putting my fingers instinctively to my cheek.

'It looks as though it was *something*.' He gestures to the seat beside me. 'Is this one free?'

I nod. As he sits down, I inhale a lungful of his aftershave – something expensive and musky that hadn't caught me back at the shop, where he hadn't been quite so close. With him sitting next to me, I feel the overwhelming nervousness that had crept over me earlier at the store. Our hips are nearly touching. I don't know where to rest my hands, or where my gaze should fall, so like an idiot I stare at the back of the seat in front of me, as though by feigning a lack of interest I might be able to disguise just how attracted I am to this stranger.

'Do you want to talk about it? This "nothing" incident?'

'I was leaving work. It was just some kid.'

'Just some kid? And he did this to you?'

'Not directly,' I tell him, looking at him now. 'He grabbed my bag... there was a scuffle. I fell and hit my face. I think it must have been a latch on a gate or something.'

'Did he steal your bag?' he asks, glancing to the floor. 'Have you called the police?'

'Honestly, I don't want the fuss.'

He studies me for a moment, his attention resting on the

tear on my cheek that's been stinging my skin relentlessly since I fell. 'You need to get that seen to. It looks like it might need gluing. You don't want it to get infected.'

'It'll be okay,' I tell him. 'I'll clean it up when I get home.'

He looks as though he's about to say something else but then thinks better of it.

'This train's a nightmare,' he comments, as a man bumps a suitcase into his legs as he searches for a free seat. 'Do you do this every day?'

'Not every day, thankfully.'

My voice leaves my body sounding nothing like my own. I don't know what's happened to me. None of my exes ever had this effect on me when we first met – and they certainly didn't provoke this reaction once we'd got to know one another. When I think about it though, I never met any of them in this way, as strangers. The two long-term relationships I've had were both with people I'd already known: one was a friend of a friend who I'd spent time with as a teenager; the other was a man I used to work with.

'I don't go into the city much if I can avoid it,' he tells me. 'It's too hectic for me.'

I wonder what he does for work, this good-looking man, who doesn't like the busyness of a city that's not all that big. I glance at his hands. His fingers look soft, uncalloused: I doubt his work involves manual labour. He's obviously not a city worker either. The mystery of him is almost as attractive as he is.

'How long have you been where you are?'

I glance at my phone. 'Only about ten minutes or so.'

The smile that stretches his mouth is infectious, like a laugh that gets caught and passed around a room. 'I meant at your work.'

'Oh my God... of course you did.'

We laugh together at my mistake, and the moment feels oddly familiar in its ease. He has beautiful creases at the corner of his eyes when he laughs. As though both sensing the easiness of the moment, we fall into a silence that sits in stark contrast.

'You might have said five years, and then I'd be wondering just how awful this train journey really is,' he teases. 'I haven't even introduced myself.' He holds his hand out to me, and I take it. His fingers feel warm against mine.

'I'm Andrew,' he says. 'Nice to meet you again, Daisy.'

And though it's only been a few hours since he read the name on my work badge, I'm struck by the fact that he's remembered it. That I mattered enough in that moment for my name to stick.

'My stop's the one after this,' he tells me. 'My car's at the park and ride. Please let me drive you to the hospital. You should get checked over.'

'That's kind of you,' I tell him, 'but I'm okay, honestly.'

I don't know this man. I'm not going to get into a car with him, no matter how thoughtful or kind he may appear to be. I'm pretty sure there's still some antiseptic cream in my bathroom cupboard. If not, there's a convenience shop just around the corner that might have something. After a clean-up, I'm sure the cut will be fine. It probably looks worse than it is.

'That's sensible. I'm sorry... you don't know me. It's none of my business.' He looks at my injury with concern. 'I'm guessing this "kid" who did this to you was male, am I right?'

I nod.

'Okay. Well, on behalf of the male population, young, old and somewhere in between, I'd like to prove to you that we're not all total shits. If you'll let me. I'm not going to ask for your number, but would it be okay if I give you mine? And if you don't want to ever make any use of it, that's fine as well.'

I feel as though I'm in some kind of romcom. A meeting

with a stranger in a workplace... a chance encounter on a journey home. Things like this don't happen to women like me.

And yet, somehow, here it is... happening.

FOUR

With my house key stolen, I can't get into my flat. Fortunately, a crazy night out with Aisha during which she managed to lose half her personal belongings despite being stone-cold sober was a lesson to me to leave a spare with a neighbour. There's already one with Craig in the flat downstairs, but he also happens to be the landlord and a horrible human being, and I would rather spend the night on a park bench than ask him for help. Instead, the person I chose to trust with a spare key is a woman in one of the terraces across the street who lives alone with a brood of cats and doesn't seem to have much of a social life.

'I'm sorry to interrupt you so late,' I say, as she opens her front door. The television sounds out from the living room with the tinny theme tune of a popular game show.

'My God, what's happened to you?'

'Long story,' I say, trying to brush off her concern.

'I have time,' she says, gesturing to the crochet pattern she's holding in her left hand. 'I'm making a wool poodle... I have all the time in the world.'

She gestures for me to go inside, so I step in and shut the front door behind me.

'I've lost my key,' I tell her.

'You need the spare? It's in here somewhere.'

I linger on the welcome mat as she riffles through her hallway set of drawers.

'What happened, love? Have you been mugged?'

'How did you know?'

She stops what she's doing and looks at me. 'Cut-up face… no bag… lost keys. Just call me Jessica Fletcher.'

'Who?'

'Oh my God, you're so young. Or I'm so old. Never mind. Is this the one?'

She holds up a key on a small metal keyring shaped like a reindeer head, one I'd pulled from a cracker at a Christmas works do years ago. 'That's it,' I say, taking it from her. 'Thank you.'

'Make sure you report it. Bastard shouldn't get away with it. You're going to need to get that lock changed now, too.'

'Thank you,' I say again. I just want to get into the flat now. I'm tired and my head's hurting.

'If you need anything, love, you know where I am.'

I don't hear her door close as I step on to the pavement and make my way across the street, and I imagine her standing there watching me pitifully. The thought strikes me with its irony. I've judged my neighbour in the past. How old is she? She could be anywhere between forty-five and sixty-five, one of those people that's hard to place. Alone with her cats, doing crochet on a Thursday evening, I might have pitied her for her quiet, mundane life. Yet she seems happy. Contented.

I wish I could claim the same.

I let myself into the front door and scoop up all the post. Craig is too bone idle to pick it up. I don't know why I'd ever expected him to sort out the flat's damp problem when he can't even pick up his post from the mat. Upstairs, the place seems eerily quiet. I plug my phone into its charger and play some music while I go to the bathroom to clean up my face. The cut on my cheek stings as I wash it out. I find some antiseptic cream in the cupboard and take a couple of paracetamols for the headache that's raging at my temples.

I write Aisha a text telling her about it, but I delete it before sending. She's got enough on her plate with looking after her aging grandparents, and I don't want to worry her. In the bedroom, I change from my work clothes into a pair of comfy pyjamas. I could climb into bed already, despite it not yet being eight thirty, though I doubt I would get any sleep. I feel wired with adrenaline and anger. If I'd just left work a bit earlier... if I hadn't hung about checking my emails and then lingering on that rejection.

But it's all futile. I left when I did, and what happened, happened.

I go back through the living room and into the kitchen, make myself a cup of tea and take it to the sofa. With the television turned to a dating show where people judge each other on menus, I check my phone, still lingering on the thought of texting Aisha while knowing that I won't. *You could message Andrew*, a voice inside my head tells me, but I quickly dismiss the idea as ridiculous.

Eventually, I drift into a restless, dream-filled sleep. I find myself in a crowd of people. There is a beat, repetitive and familiar, played loudly. The air is hot and thick and there are bodies everywhere, people dancing and jostling, weaving around one another to get to the bar or to the side of the boat – to take in the beautiful views of the Mediterranean ocean, stretched and glistening beneath the baking sun.

And then there is an explosion.

It should rip me from my sleep, as it has done so many times before. Instead, I am thrown sideways into him as the boat tilts wildly. My head hits something, dizzying me. He reaches for my hand, and I take it. He pulls me up, just as the deck above us collapses in on itself, crashing around us in a cloud of beams and metal, dust and glass.

There are flames from behind the debris... dance music still pulsing from the speakers, as though the party remains in full swing. As though the boat isn't filling with water. As though the two of us aren't stuck here, trapped, the water surging onboard as the people out on deck scream and panic and try to scrabble for a temporary safety.

I reach for his hand and squeeze his fingers between mine, silently praying to a God I'm cynical about at best, promising I will do better, if I can only be given a chance to.

I hear his voice in my dream as it came to me then: distant beyond the noise.

My leg. Help me... it's trapped.

I am faced with a choice: to leave him, or to try to save myself.

The water is rising around us. We are going to drown.

FIVE

The following morning, I wake up with the kind of headache that comes from broken and disturbed sleep. When I open my eyes, I can still see the water rising. I can still feel it, freezing around my thighs. The nightmare comes less frequently now, but when it does, it's still as sharp and vivid as it ever was. There's a tightening around my heart that always follows it, as though my circulation is being strangled. I can't breathe. It's like being submerged all over again.

I'm still in the living room with my lower back arched uncomfortably on the ridge between two of the sofa cushions. I reach to the floor for my phone. On a workday, this would be sleeping in late, but I've nothing to get up for this morning.

'Shit.'

I sit up sharply, and the pain in my head surges like a wave, threatening to knock me sideways. I go through the kitchen to the bathroom at the back of the flat, where I assess the damage to my face. It somehow manages to look even worse this morning. The cut on my cheek is outlined with a sickly green bruise, shaped like an oversized kidney bean like one of those cardboard bowls they give you in hospital to throw up in.

At the thought, a rush of bile rises in my throat. I open the toilet lid in time, and after my stomach has been purged, it occurs to me that I'm not sure when I last ate something. I flush the toilet and sit on the closed lid with my head in my hands, feeling as though I sank two bottles of wine last night. And at the thought of sinking, the details of my nightmare come back like the rise of a tide, threatening to sweep me once again beneath its surface.

I brush my teeth before going into the kitchen for a glass of water. At the window, where the 'picturesque view' described by my landlord is actually the brickwork of the house next door, I think about reporting what happened yesterday to the police. When I went over it in my mind last night, I reasoned with myself that there was nothing they'd be able to do about it: there are no CCTV cameras beyond the boundary of the delivery area, and my attacker either knew this, or he was lucky to find me where he did. Or should it be that I was unlucky? There are no details I can offer about his age or appearance; it was too dark for me to be able to tell the police anything. Going to them seemed pointless.

But this morning, I'm not so sure. If I don't report it, it feels as though I'm just giving in to what happened. The perpetrator will likely still get away with it, but at least I'll have done something, even if it turns out to be futile. If he's worked out that the lane is potentially a hot spot for robbing people without chance of any repercussion, he might attempt to do the same again. It could happen to someone I work with. It could happen to Aisha.

If I do nothing, I'm as good as responsible.

I'll go to the police station. But I don't want to go there alone.

The last time I had any involvement with the police, it had felt like an attack: a barrage of questions fired at me one after the other, none of which I'd felt able to answer. I was still at the hospital, still dazed and disorientated from what now felt like a nightmare – something I'd lived through, yet didn't somehow seem real. Every question had sounded like a challenge; every look had felt like an accusation. I wasn't responsible for what had happened. And yet, somehow still, I was. I was the one who'd suggested we go down to the seating area below deck. If we'd stayed outside with everyone else, things might have ended so differently. And the police had looked at me as if it was all my fault.

I can't face them again now on my own.

In the living room, I retrieve my phone from the floor and pull up Aisha's number. It rings for a while, and I'm about to hang up when she answers.

'Daisy. I meant to text you.'

'Everything okay?'

'No, not really. It's Dada. He's back in hospital.'

Aisha's grandfather, or 'Dada' as she affectionately calls him, has been in and out of hospital over the past year or so, having suffered a series of mini strokes. The effects on his balance and coordination led to several falls, and at the start of the year Aisha moved in with her grandparents to help with their care. Even when things have been at their most difficult, I've rarely seen Aisha without a smile on her face. But recently, it's been obvious things are taking their toll.

'What happened?'

'He fell in the kitchen. Hit his head on the corner of the worktop.'

'Oh no, I'm so sorry. What have they said? Is he okay?'

'It could have been a lot worse. But it's just a matter of time now, you know?'

The doctors have warned Aisha and her nana that mini strokes can often lead to a major stroke. They know they're living on borrowed time, waiting for the inevitable.

'Is there anything I can do?' I ask her. 'Do you need anything?'

'I don't think so. But thank you. I'm obviously going to have to take a rain check on tonight.'

'Of course.'

There's no way I'm going to bother Aisha with the attack considering what she and her grandparents are going through. It's so insignificant in comparison.

'Look, if you need anything later, I can bring over shopping or make some food.'

'Thanks. I don't know how long we're going to be here, or how long he'll be in though.'

'Okay. Let me know how he's doing later, if you're able to. Give them both my love.'

'Everything okay with you?'

'Yeah, fine,' I lie. 'I'll text you later. Make sure you eat something.'

'Okay, Auntie Daisy,' she jokes.

After we end the call, I go for a shower. I feel better once I've washed my hair, as though I've washed away what happened last night. I apply some make-up, realising it won't be enough to conceal the cut on my face and the bruising that has developed beneath my left eye.

I start trying to compose a text, but everything I write is either overly familiar or standoffish, with no middle ground to be found. I don't want to come across as too keen, but I don't want to appear abrupt either. After repeatedly typing and deleting, I settle on something that seems friendly without being over the top and doesn't demand a response.

Hi Andrew. It's Daisy. Thanks for your concern yesterday. Face much better this morning – looked worse than it was.

With the phone in my hand and the text written but unsent,

I sit and consider all the reasons not to send it. Perhaps he was just being friendly and wanted to help me yesterday after seeing me injured. Now that I'm okay, maybe he won't want to hear from me. I might have mistaken his sympathy as something else... though when his gaze sent a spark fizzing through me yesterday at the store, I'd wondered whether he'd felt the same.

I quickly press the send button, and then I wait.

SIX

The residents are all in the dining room when I arrive at the home at just gone 1 p.m. I wait out in the hallway and watch Liam through the door, struck as always by the cruelty of his circumstances. I'm not sure there's a person here who's able to eat anything more than brown pureed sludge spoon-fed by a carer. Liam has a feeding tube. I suppose that in bringing them all together at mealtimes, the staff are trying to maintain some kind of routine for the patients and for themselves. Yet it still feels like a kind of cruelty, to make him sit for something he cannot have.

Time hasn't made seeing him like this any easier. In all these years, I don't think there's been a single visit when I've not stopped at the doorway to whatever room he's been in and taken a moment to compose myself before Liam has seen me. I have fought back tears. On the days when they've defeated me, I've had to go to another room to wait for them to pass before I've gone to see him. I have worn a mask and performed a role, desperate to keep my reaction to seeing him as he is now away from him. And there have been days when I've arrived here, seen him through a window or doorway, and left without him knowing that I've been here.

Today, I go into the dining room and wave to Liam, but though I know he sees me, he doesn't respond. He can't, even if he wanted to. But I know now that he does – and can – want to communicate with me. For months after the accident, nobody was sure whether Liam was conscious of what was going on around him. There were so many tests and investigations while the medical experts tried to assess how much of Liam remained. People spoke about him as though he wasn't in the room with us.

But then one day, I saw in his eyes that he was there, still. I'm not sure what caused it; to anyone else he didn't appear to be different. But I knew in my heart that he was still with us, and while there was a chance, I was willing to try anything to find a way to break him free of the prison he'd been incarcerated in.

'Hi, Liam,' I say, as I take off my coat and hang it on the back of the chair next to his. 'It's cold out there today.'

I'm talking about the weather. It's usually an hour or so before the subject of rainfall or the temperature arises, but today we're straight to it, and I know it's going to be one of those visits during which I struggle to find things to talk to him about. One-sided conversations are difficult to sustain.

'Would you like to talk today?'

Two eye blinks in quick succession. No. It's been like this a lot recently. I've gone over and over our last conversation, trying to look for clues as to what I might have said or done wrong. I've upset him, but I don't know how.

'I've just been to the shops,' I tell him. 'Nothing exciting... just a food shop. They're packed already. Makes you wonder how busy it's going to be by Christmas.'

This is what I was told I should do, five years ago after

Liam's accident. Talk to him as you normally would, the doctors told me. And goodness knows, I've tried. But nothing has been normal since our lives were turned upside down, and though I know for sure now that he hears and understands me, and that the boy he once was continues to remain present inside his broken shell, trapped, I can never speak to him as I might have. I try to be as normal as possible around him, yet I avoid any topic that might upset or worry him. Sometimes, it leaves little for me to talk about. Every topic is tinged with a bittersweet lament... every subject is soured with his absence. How can I talk to him about the everyday occurrences of my life when he is stuck in this place, trapped inside a body that won't allow him to live as he once did, with the memories of a life that has been lost?

How can I speak to him so casually, knowing the ways in which I failed him?

'Hello,' a voice behind me says. 'You're early this week.'

I turn to see one of the nurses, Kathleen, carrying a bag of medication.

'I was missing him,' I say, taking Liam's hand and squeezing it gently in mine.

Kathleen gives me a double look before leaning to speak quietly into one of the other patient's ears. She takes the brake off his wheelchair and turns him to face the door.

'Would you like to go into the lounge?' she asks me.

'I think I'll take Liam up to his room, if that's okay.'

'Of course. Someone will be coming round with tea in about twenty minutes.'

I thank her and take my coat from the back of the seat before hanging it over the handles of Liam's wheelchair. I push him from the dining room and out into the hallway, and we go up in the lift to his first-floor bedroom. The radio on his bedside table has been left on, and a male voice quietly relates the details of a train crash that happened in the early hours of this morning somewhere up in Yorkshire. I switch it off and turn

Liam's chair so that he's facing the window, then I slide the visitor chair beside him so I can sit and hold his hand while we watch a robin land on the windowsill to nibble at the birdseed in the feeder I hung there during the summer.

'How pretty,' I say. 'It's like a Christmas card.'

The room is too hot. Or maybe it's just me. I feel sweaty and uncomfortable, wishing I'd worn something more than just a vest top beneath the heavy jumper I'm now stuck wearing. I should have known not to choose it to wear here; the place is always like a sauna.

'Are you too warm?' I ask. I wait for a blink, or maybe two, but he offers me nothing.

'I'm sorry if I've upset you. I keep going over what we talked about a few weeks back, but I can't work out what I said wrong. I'm doing my best. I know it doesn't count for much.'

His fingers are like ice against mine, answering my question for him.

'I'm going to make everything right,' I tell him. 'You just need to trust me, okay? Everything is going to be all right.'

I put a hand to his head and push an unruly wisp of hair behind his ear. It feels slippery with grease.

'Is there anything you need?' I ask him.

I expect nothing in response, but I get a single eye blink. Yes.

'What?' I ask stupidly, as though it's easy enough for him to give me an instant answer. I get up and go to the drawer where his letter boards are kept. Six months after the accident, I managed to convince the medical professionals who'd been caring for Liam that he was still with us, still able to hear and understand what was going on around us. I couldn't comprehend how terrifying it must have been for him. People had been talking about ending his life, with him lying there next to them, unable to intervene and tell them that he was still here.

A little less than a year after the accident, I started to help

Liam to communicate with me. I'd spent a lot of time reading over those past few months – medical journals and research papers, accounts from family members of other victims of locked-in syndrome. I joined online forums and spoke anonymously to other people in similar situations to ours, gathering information on how I could help Liam to in some way rejoin the world around him. It was a shock to find that although the condition is rare, there were so many people affected by it. Family, friends, colleagues... we all mean so much to more people than we probably realise.

I researched the methods that family members and professionals had used to 'free' patients to be able to communicate. Using eye blinks, we quickly discovered that Liam was able to answer basic questions. The realisation that he was still with us was bittersweet. The selfish part of me was relieved to have him here. Another part feared the kind of life he'd been condemned to.

'Tell me,' I say, tapping the first of the letter boards. 'Whatever it is you need, please just tell me, okay?'

I run a finger slowly along the first set of letters, which are arranged according to how frequently they are used in the English language. I run my finger past E, then T, and as we continue, my focus remains fixed on Liam's eyes as I wait for a blink.

I start on the second board. He blinks, once.

Yes.

I look at the letter where my finger rests. G.

I continue the pattern, returning to the first board. A single blink comes quickly, when my finger rests at the O.

On we go, until we have six letters.

G O H O M E.

Go home.

The words cut through me like a blade, though I try not to let any reaction slip to my face.

Okay,' I say, almost choking on the tears that threaten to spill over. 'If that's what you want.'

I get my coat, and I go back to him, planting a kiss on his forehead before telling him that I love him. I leave him staring at the window, from where the little robin that had graced us with its presence earlier on is now long gone.

'I'll be back next week,' I say to his back. 'I love you, Liam. I'm sorry.'

I slip away quickly, not wanting him to hear my tears. In the day room just along the corridor, I dump my coat on to one of the empty chairs and sit in the next with my head in my hands, wondering what's gone so wrong these last few visits that Liam now doesn't want me here at all.

'Everything okay, love?'

Kathleen appears at the doorway. She has been here for as long as Liam has, one of the first nurses to treat him after he moved into the unit. She tilts her head, concern etching her small features. 'You look exhausted.'

'Just one of those nights last night,' I say casually, hoping to steer her attention in a different direction. I don't want to tell her that Liam has asked me to leave. I know the nurses here also use the letter boards to communicate with him, and now I wonder what he says about me when I'm not here.

She comes into the room and puts a hand on my sleeve. 'You're doing a great job. Make sure you're looking after yourself too though, love.' She gives my arm a reassuring rub before heading to the neighbouring room, while I stay sitting where I am, stung by her kindness.

Because no matter what anyone tells me, I don't deserve it.

In my coat pocket, my phone pings, snapping me from self-pity. I pick up my things and leave the unit, only checking the message once I'm outside the building. It's from Andrew.

SEVEN

The following Wednesday, I wait in the communal hallway downstairs for the Uber to arrive, giving myself a final mirror check as I keep an eye on the route update that lets me know how far away my driver is. Google tells me that the restaurant Andrew has chosen for tonight is six miles from where I live. Despite the relatively short distance, it will still take over an hour to get there by train. It's only twenty minutes by car though, so I order an Uber, excusing the extravagance by convincing myself that with the walks to and from each train station thrown in, I'm likely to be late, and I don't want to be late for a first date. Andrew had asked if I'd like to choose where we meet, but it had felt like too much pressure. I don't eat out at nice restaurants, but maybe this is something Andrew does often. I wouldn't want to be judged for making a poor choice or want the responsibility of having chosen somewhere with terrible food.

'You want to be careful.'

I turn at Craig's voice, my stomach flipping at the way he looks me up and down. He's leaning against the doorframe of the downstairs flat, wearing stained jogging bottoms and a T-shirt that's too tight around his gut.

'Pardon?' I pull at the hem of my short black dress – the reliable wardrobe staple that's seen me through many nights out.

'Going out dressed like that,' he says. 'You might attract the wrong type of attention.'

I'm trying to think of a witty response when my phone pings with a notification that the Uber is outside, and when I leave the house, I feel Craig's eyes still on me, watching me go. Thankfully, the driver isn't chatty. I don't know what I'd make small talk about, and the idea of this sets off a chain of panic about how I'm supposed to get through the next few hours on a date with someone I don't know and have prior to tonight spent little more than half an hour with. When we pull on to the high street in the village of Pontyclun, I'm reassured that the restaurant isn't going to be too fancy or expensive. The window is lit with pretty fairy lights, giving the place a welcoming glow. When I pull the front door open, I'm greeted with the smell of garlic and herbs. I check my reflection in the glass of the front window, conscious of the cut on my face that I'm starting to think might scar. I tried to cover it with concealer and foundation, but it's still more visible than I'd like it to be.

I wait a moment for a member of staff to greet me, and for these seconds that feel like hours I stand awkwardly self-conscious, my eyes flitting around the room as I try to spot Andrew among the diners. What if he's not here? It's happened to me once before, when I was in my late teens, and I'd made a promise I'd never let myself be put in that position again. But maybe I've just walked right into a repeat scenario.

A young woman heads over to me from the bar area just as I'm contemplating walking back out of the building. What am I doing here? I've never been on a date with someone I don't know before, and I'm already anticipating the effect I know this man is going to have on me.

'Have you booked a table?' she asks, the words swirled on a gorgeous Italian accent. She carries an iPad and glances down at what I assume are the evening's bookings.

'Yes. Well, no... not in my name. It's Andrew—' But I stop abruptly, realising I've never asked his surname. I've not yet been able to look him up on social media; I wouldn't have been able to ask for his surname without it looking obvious that this was what I intended to do.

'Andrew Miller,' the young woman says, scrolling the iPad. 'He's already here. Follow me, please.'

And now it's too late to leave because I'm following her into the restaurant's dining area, weaving our way between tables until I see him in a far corner, sitting beneath a gallery of artworks all in ornate gold frames of different shapes and sizes. He stands when he sees us approaching. Old-fashioned manners, as Aisha's nana would say. Surely a keeper.

'Daisy,' he says, with that way of saying my name that makes it sound like no one else ever has. 'You look lovely.'

'Thank you.' I wonder if I'm supposed to say something complimentary back, but my tongue has swollen in my mouth and every possible reply seems stupid. Instead I say nothing and just smile as I wriggle out of my coat.

We give the waitress our drinks order, and then we're alone, leaving me feeling even more self-conscious.

'Nice choice of restaurant,' I say, as I turn to hang my coat on the back of my chair. 'Love the artwork.'

'The food's always amazing here.'

My heart sinks a bit. I wonder how many dates he's been on in this same place; how many women he's met through the art of apparent casual conversation. Perhaps he picks up dates like other men buy coffees, and I'm just one in a succession of nights out.

'This is looking so much better already.' He gestures to his own cheek.

'It looked worse than it was.'

'Did you report it to the police?'

I shake my head and reach for a menu, looking for a distraction from the subject of the assault. 'What do you usually order?'

I sense him looking at me with that same raised eyebrow stare he'd given me on the train when I'd told him I hadn't needed to go to the hospital. 'I usually choose something from the specials.' He points to a wall-mounted chalkboard on the far wall behind me. When I turn back, that look on his face remains in place.

'It's not too late to report it.'

'I don't want to.'

Silence falls between us at the curtness of my words, which come out far more bluntly than I'd meant them to.

'I'm sorry,' Andrew says. 'It isn't my business to pry.' He turns when he notices me looking at something behind him. 'Seen anything you like the look of?' he asks. There's a glint in his eye. 'The artwork, I mean,' he adds, gesturing to the gallery behind him.

'The one there,' I tell him, hoping the flush I can feel rising in my cheeks isn't visible. I point to a print of a man and woman running across a road at the end of a street lined with terraced houses. Something in their urgency and untold story keeps me fixated on the details of the brush strokes. 'It's just got something about it, hasn't it? Looks a bit like the street where I grew up.'

'Where was that?'

'Tonypandy. To be fair, the streets all sort of look the same.'

We're interrupted when the waitress returns with our drinks: a glass of white wine for me; a red for Andrew.

'What?' he says, a smile curling at the corner of his lips as he gauges the expression on my face as the waitress walks away from our table.

'I've never been on a date with a man who drinks wine,' I admit.

'Really? That makes me curious about who you've been dating.'

Andrew is so confident. So self-assured. Yet there's not a shred of arrogance about him... not yet, at least. I remind myself that just because it hasn't yet shown itself, that doesn't mean it doesn't exist.

'No one, actually. Not for a long time.'

'Am I allowed to ask why that is?'

'You're allowed to ask,' I tell him, 'but I'm not obligated to answer.'

He smiles. 'Of course not. You're welcome to leave me wondering.'

Like at the department store last week, the flirtation levels are high. When he takes a drink, I find myself looking for too long at his lips, distracted by the thought of what they might taste like.

'What do you do for a job?' I ask, feeling the heat in my face begin to surge again.

'I work in data security. And yes... it's as boring as it sounds.'

'How long have you done that?'

'What feels like forever.'

He sets his drink back on the table, and I can't help but notice the way his eyes don't leave me as he does so. His eyes are beautiful, dark with bronze flecks running through his irises, and his lashes are enviable, thick and dark.

We order food, and while we wait, the conversation flows easily, from our jobs to our homes, to a Netflix series we've both recently watched. By the time our meals have been eaten, and we've shared a massively-portioned slice of tiramisu, my stomach is full of calories and my heart is full of the kind of butterflies I've not felt since I was thirteen and wildly in love with the boy who worked behind the counter at the corner shop on the next street from my home.

My head is already full of Andrew, and as I listen to him laugh his way through an anecdote involving a former colleague and an unfortunately selected 'secret Santa' gift, I feel myself consumed by this man who is so unlike anyone I've ever dated before.

By the time we reach the end of a second bottle of wine, the restaurant staff are cleaning up around us, and it's only now I realise that we're the last customers here.

'Could I get the bill please?' Andrew asks a waiter as he goes to wipe down the table closest to ours.

I reach for my bag and take out my phone, slipping my bank card from inside its case.

'Absolutely not,' Andrew insists, putting out a hand. 'This is my treat.'

'That's kind of you, but I'd rather pay my own way.'

'And I appreciate that. But it would make me happy if you let me pay. You don't want to see me unhappy, do you?'

He shoots me a smile as the waiter returns with the bill and a card reader. I let him pay, resolving to pay on the next date, should it happen that he wants to see me again after tonight. I order an Uber, and we wait inside the doorway for it to arrive.

'Thank you,' Andrew says. 'For tonight. I've had a lovely time.'

'Me too.'

'I'd love to do it again sometime… if that's something you'd like too.'

'Definitely. I'd love to.'

I see a car pull up across the street, and as we step outside the restaurant, a blast of cold air cuts through my coat. It makes me suddenly aware of how much I've had to drink.

'Daisy,' Andrew says, taking my hand in his and pulling me back from the kerb. Standing now just inches from him, I realise he must be at least half a foot taller than my five foot five. I'm so close I can see the pores of his skin above his stubbled jawline... the small silver scar that runs from the curve of his nose to the middle of his cheek.

'Can I kiss you?'

I don't think anyone's ever asked me this before; it's usually just happened, more often than not awkwardly, the result of too much alcohol, or a fumbled, end-of-the-night parting gesture that has rarely lived up to its expectation.

'Would you like to kiss me?'

Without saying anything else, he reaches for my face, the fingers of his right hand brushing across my cheek like a whisper. They move to my hair, and then he lowers his face to mine. His lips taste of red wine, and as his tongue finds mine, I feel his left arm snake around my waist, pulling me in closer. A shock of electricity rushes the length of my body.

Never go home with someone on the first night, I hear Aisha's voice remind me. *You never know who's a serial killer.*

And though I know she's right, Andrew's the only first date I've ever been tempted to break the rule for.

EIGHT

Despite Aisha's aversion to quiet nights in, that Saturday we find ourselves at my flat. Our night out last week had been postponed because of her Dada's fall, but with Yousuf now back at home after his stay in hospital, we arranged to meet up. The weather has been terrible all afternoon, the rain relentless, so I texted Aisha earlier to suggest a takeaway and a film we know neither of us will watch because we'll be too busy talking over it. For once, the prospect of a night in seems more appealing to both of us than it might have just a week ago.

I spent the afternoon cleaning the flat, powered by music I turned up too loudly and thoughts of Andrew I allowed myself to linger on too intensely. I can't remember the last time I was so attracted to a man, or whether I've even been so drawn to someone in the way I am to him. That kiss. My God... that kiss. It felt like being a teenager again.

I messaged him that night to let him know I'd got home safely, and there followed a succession of texts that made it clear we were both keen to see each other again.

'So come on,' Aisha says, tucking her legs beneath her at the other end of the sofa. 'Let's hear all about it.'

'All about what?'

'Oh, stop it,' she says teasingly, raising the cup of tea I've made her to her lips. 'Mr Perfume. I want to know everything. With details.' She grins. 'Okay... maybe not all the details.'

'There was nothing like that,' I tell her. 'Sorry to disappoint you.'

Her eyebrows stretch into arches. 'How very boring.'

'Not yet at least.'

She laughs.

There's a loud bang from the flat downstairs. 'What was that?' Aisha asks, putting her mug on the table beside her.

'God knows. There's always weird noises coming from down there.'

'You'll be seeing him again then?' she redirects the conversation.

I nod. 'He's not like anyone I've ever met before.'

'In what way?'

'I don't know. He's a man, I suppose. The others all seem like little boys by comparison.'

'How old is he?'

'Thirty-nine.'

'That'll be why then. He's practically middle-aged.'

I laugh. 'Not quite. And anyway... it's just around the corner, you know.'

'Nah. Not for me. I'm forever twenty-seven. I'm refusing to get old.' The smile fades from her lips as she reaches for her tea, and I know her thoughts have shifted from my date to her grandfather, suddenly so much older and less able than he'd been just eighteen months ago.

'How's your dada been since he got home?'

She shrugs. 'Much the same. Every day seems to get a bit harder for him now. I hate seeing him like this. I hate seeing the effect it's having on Nana.'

I reach over and put a hand on her arm. 'They're lucky to have you.'

'I don't know about that. I can't change anything.'

'No one can do that. But no one could do more than you're doing, either.'

Aisha's eyes glisten with tears. I don't think I've ever seen her so close to crying before. Her approach to most situations is to crack a joke and carry on, regardless of whatever's going on in her life.

'The mood was better when we were talking about Mr Perfume.' She wipes a hand across her eye, smudging her eyeliner at the corner. 'So when are you seeing him next?'

'He's offered to cook for me tomorrow.'

Our chat is interrupted by a scream. It's so loud it makes Aisha jump, and tea slops from the mug into her lap.

'Are you okay?' I ask, wondering how hot the drink still is, and whether it might have burned her through her clothes.

'I'm sorry. I'll get a tea towel.'

'Don't worry about that. Are you burned?'

'No, I'm fine.'

'What the hell was that?' I muse.

'I don't know... you're the one who said there's always weird noises coming from down there.'

'But not like that.' A creeping sense of unease travels through my veins. The bangs and thuds are not unusual, and loud music often thumps through the floorboards from the flat downstairs, but I've never heard a scream like that before.

'What?' Aisha asks, seeing the look on my face. 'What's wrong?'

'I just don't like the sound of that.'

It was a woman's voice, the scream high-pitched and distressed. But it's now the silence that's bothering me even more.

Aisha reaches to the floor for her handbag and takes out her mobile phone.

'What are you doing?'

'Calling the police.'

'What? No. I mean... It's probably nothing.'

Aisha's left eyebrow raises. 'You've told me plenty of times before that there's something off about your landlord,' she reminds me. 'Would you rather chance it and find out something terrible's happened?'

She's right; I've told her on plenty of occasions what a creep I think Craig is. I wouldn't forgive myself if I found out that scream had been a signal of something sinister, and I'd reacted to it by doing nothing. Yet calling the police seems a bit extreme.

'We could just go down there and see,' I suggest.

But it's too late: Aisha is already connected to emergency services and is now giving the call handler my address. I realise how much shit this could get me into. Craig might be a pervy oddball, but this flat is the best I'm able to afford for now, and if he kicks me out for calling the police, I've got nowhere else to go.

'Aisha,' I hiss, but she bats a hand before putting her mobile on the coffee table and getting down on the floor. She reaches for the glass I gave her earlier, now empty, and places it upside down on the laminate floor. She presses her ear to the glass.

'I'm not sure that really works,' I start to object, but a moment later she's reached for her phone again and is telling the person at the other end of the call that whatever the noises are, they're definitely coming from downstairs.

'She said they'll send someone round to check,' she says, after the call has been ended.

'And it'll probably be nothing. Just the TV turned up too loud, or something.'

Her eyebrow arches. 'That wasn't the TV. And anyway, if it's nothing then we can sleep well tonight, can't we?'

We sit uneasily for the next twenty minutes or so, while Aisha deliberates the possibility that someone downstairs might be hurt, and while I worry what the repercussions of this might be for me if it turns out we've made a mistake.

'They're taking too long,' she says, standing from the sofa. 'I'm going to go down there.'

'What? No... you can't.'

'It's gone too quiet. If someone's hurt and we do nothing, we'll never forgive ourselves. Come on.'

I admire Aisha's sense of moral responsibility, but I'm equally wary of Craig's hostility. I once saw him shove a dog shit through a crack in the window of a car that kept parking outside the house.

'It'll be fine,' she says, sensing my unease. 'What's he going to do with two of us there?'

She heads downstairs, and I have little other choice than to follow. In the shared hallway, she knocks on the door of the downstairs flat. When it goes unanswered, she knocks again, louder this time.

Moments later, Craig answers the door. We're greeted by an expanse of pale, soft flesh in the form of his naked stomach and chest. A black and white Pepé Le Pew tattoo winks suggestively at me beneath a scroll that says 'Mum', the strangeness of the placement clearly lost on this human canvas of graffiti.

'What?'

'We just wanted to check everything's okay,' Aisha says. 'We heard a scream.'

'Must have been next door,' he says, staring at her chest.

'I don't think so,' Aisha says, and as much as I love her, I wish she'd stop talking. 'I'm pretty sure it came from down here.'

He shrugs. 'Sorry... can't help you.'

Behind us, there's a knock at the front door. My heart sinks with the thought that it might be the police. If it is, and we've overreacted to something innocent, I'm going to be looking for somewhere new to live.

Craig shoves past us to answer the door. I'm hit with the mess that lies beyond his door. Bottles and wrappers litter the living room floor, and there's a smell like wet dog that hangs like a curtain in the doorway.

'We've received a report of screaming coming from your flat.'

The officer looks too young – like he's come straight from police training college, though it makes sense they wouldn't send their most experienced officers to deal with unidentified screams that could still possibly turn out to be someone's TV.

'Come on in,' Craig says, with a smirk on his face that suggests he might be enjoying himself. 'I'm sorry your time's been wasted like this.'

'Do you live here?' The officer gestures to the downstairs flat.

Craig nods. 'I'm the landlord. Daisy rents upstairs.'

'You reported the noise?' the officer asks me.

'I did,' Aisha says quickly.

'You're welcome to come and take a look,' Craig says to the officer.

'You didn't need to say that,' I whisper when the two men go into the flat.

'What? It was me who called them.'

She puts her head to the wall to try to listen in on them.

'How long do we wait?' Aisha asks. 'What if he doesn't come back out?'

I roll my eyes. 'You watch too much Netflix.'

A minute or so later, the young officer appears back in the hallway. His face is flushed pink. Behind him, Craig has thankfully put a T-shirt on, and Pepé Le Pew has subsequently been decapitated.

'Everything's sorted,' the officer says awkwardly. He turns to Craig. 'Thanks for your cooperation.'

Craig swears beneath his breath before going back into his flat and slamming the door shut behind him. The officer's face is now puce.

'So,' he says, 'everything is fine. You did hear a scream, but… yeah… everything is fine.'

Aisha's dark eyebrows tilt towards one another. 'So what was it then?'

'The scream? Uh… he and a lady friend were engaged in, uh…'

There's a lengthy pause before Aisha stifles a snigger, and I feel increasingly sorry for the young officer who's looking more uncomfortable by the second. 'Oh,' Aisha says, stretching the word into five syllables. 'We're talking *Fifty Shades*?'

'Something like that.'

He swiftly wraps things up by telling us we did the right thing by calling in anyway, and then the poor man can't get out of the front door quickly enough. He almost trips as he steps out into the pavement, and once I've closed the door behind him, Aisha falls into a fit of laughter.

'Oh my God,' she mouths at me, putting her hand to her face.

But my chest has tightened with anxiety, and I can't find anything to laugh about. Aisha might be finding this funny, but I'm the one stuck living here with this man in the flat underneath me. And after what happened tonight, I'm pretty sure he's not going to make life any easier for me.

NINE

Andrew sends me his address, and as any self-respecting person with the world now at their fingertips would, I tap it into my phone for a sneak preview of where I'll be spending the evening. I've never heard of Coychurch before, even though it's less than half an hour from where I live. The house is a beautiful, detached property set on its own at the bottom of a cul-de-sac, and my first thought is how any single person in their thirties is available to afford somewhere like it. I'm guessing that Andrew must have either had it passed down to him or he's been the recipient of a substantial inheritance pot, because although data security might be a respectable career, I'm sure it's not lucrative enough to fund a home that must have cost close to a million pounds.

I don't know what I'm going to wear. The last time I went on a date at anyone's house, I went Dutch on a Chinese takeaway and spent the evening curled on the sofa watching back-to-back episodes of *Line of Duty*. Whatever Andrew has planned tonight, it feels a safe bet it'll involve a three-course dinner. I can't turn up in a pair of leggings.

I get the train to Bridgend and walk the two miles from the

station to the house, following the map on my phone. The house sits among a few other equally beautiful homes, all privately gated, and Andrew's car is parked on the driveway. He answers the front door looking devastatingly handsome, his hair tousled as though he's not long come out from the shower. His shirt-sleeves are rolled up and it's unbuttoned at the neck, revealing just enough chest to offer a sneak preview of what awaits beneath.

'Come in,' he says. 'It's freezing. You haven't walked, have you?'

'Only from the station.'

'In Bridgend? You should have called – I would have picked you up.'

I slip off my coat and he takes it from me, hanging it next to his on the coat rack nailed to the wall.

'Something smells amazing.' The hallway is filled with the aromas of a home-cooked Sunday: roast potatoes and meat and honey-glazed parsnips. My stomach rumbles at the smell of it, and Andrew smiles.

'Come on through. I'm almost done.'

As we pass the living room, I take a sneaky peak inside. The walls are painted a deep blue, with minimalist white furniture. There's a large print of a seascape behind the sofa. The kitchen is equally Instagram-worthy – all steel appliances and marble work surfaces, and one of those fridges that has water and ice dispensers inbuilt in the door. Above the central island, an array of pans and utensils hang from thick wooden beams, like one of those trendy industrial open-kitchen restaurants.

'I got you this,' I say, reaching into my bag for the bottle of red I bought earlier.

He takes it from me and reads the label. 'French Malbec. Someone was paying attention at the restaurant.' He leans in and kisses me on the cheek. 'Thank you, Daisy.'

My God, he smells amazing. The thought of skipping dinner and heading straight for dessert enters my head.

Stop it, Daisy.

'Would you like a glass?' he asks, gesturing to the bottle. 'Or I've got white for you in the fridge, if you prefer.'

'I'll have white, thanks.'

He pulls a chair out from the table, and gestures for me to sit down.

'I promise it won't be long,' he tells me.

I feel as though I'm in a fancy restaurant somewhere, not in the home of someone I met while at work, then met again on the train while looking like an extra from *Fight Club*. I'm still not sure how I've managed this, or what he sees in me. Whatever the attraction is, I'm grateful for it.

'So how's your weekend been?' he asks me, as he takes a bottle of white wine from the fridge.

'Interesting.' Thankfully, I haven't seen Craig since the incident last night, and I'm hoping it stays that way.

Andrew fixes me with a look as he pulls the cork from the bottle. 'Interesting? Sounds like there's more to that.'

He brings over my wine, and as he prepares our food, I tell him what happened while Aisha was over at the flat.

'Seriously,' he says, as he places a starter of some kind of asparagus salad in front of me. 'This guy sounds a creep.'

'That looks amazing. Thank you.'

He sits opposite me. In the soft glow of the candlelight, he manages to look even more handsome than he did when he opened the front door.

We're barely into our starters when I hear a sound in the hallway. Andrew appears unfazed that there seems to be someone else in his house, and a moment later, a woman appears in the kitchen doorway. She has blonde highlighted hair that's swept back loosely from her face, soft waves falling at her cheeks. She's wearing knee-high boots and an expensive-looking caramel-coloured coat that's cinched in at her slim waist. When she smiles, her grey eyes crease at the corners with warmth.

'You must be Daisy,' she says, heading straight for me with open arms. 'I've heard so much about you.'

I glance at Andrew, whose face looks pinched, his features tightened at the interruption. The woman stops before she reaches me, moving her gaze from me to him and back again. 'He hasn't told you about me, has he?' Her lips curl into a smile. 'Andrew!' she says, with a mock scolding tone. 'Surely I'm not that much of an embarrassment to you? God, you'd think he's still thirteen.'

She extends a hand to me, and as she nears, I get a waft of her perfume. Floral.

'I'm Rachel,' she introduces herself. 'Andrew's mother.'

It's all I can do to stop my mouth from falling open. Andrew's mother hardly looks much older than he is, and she is glamorous in a way not many people can carry off. She has a movie-star look about her, all smoky-eyed make-up and photo-ready smile. Like Kim Cattrall in her *Sex and the City* days.

'Nice to meet you,' I say, still trying to quell my surprise at how young she is. Or at least, at how young she looks. Some women are genetically blessed, or able to afford ludicrously priced collagen products. Looking at Rachel's barely lined skin, I'm guessing it's one or both these things, although she doesn't look as though she's had any cosmetic surgery.

'So, it's you I need to thank,' she says.

'For...?'

'The beautiful perfume. I knew straight away Andrew hadn't chosen it.'

'I'm so glad you like it.'

'A woman can pick out what another woman will like far better than any man can,' she says with her perfect-teeth smile. 'Anyway, I won't interrupt you two any longer. I just forgot something.'

She slips past us and goes back into the hallway, and a moment later we hear her head up the stairs. Now I realise why Andrew has never mentioned his mother to me since that first meeting in the department store. It also makes sense how he manages to live in this beautiful house.

'You live with your mother?' I ask quietly, in case she overhears us on her way back downstairs.

He shakes his head. 'She lives with me. It's only a temporary thing.' He lowers his voice even more. 'She's had a few setbacks. I'm just helping her out while she arranges something more permanent.'

We fall into silence as we hear her come back down the stairs. She reappears at the doorway with an envelope in her hand.

'Have a lovely evening, both. See you again, Daisy.'

'Nice to meet you, Rachel.'

We both wait to hear the front door close before either of us speaks.

'Your mother looks so young.'

'She is, I suppose. She was only fifteen when she had me.'

Andrew pushes back his chair and gets up from the table. 'Sorry,' he says, 'just need to check the potatoes.'

But I'm pretty sure it's an excuse to get away from me for a moment. For whatever reason, Andrew seemed to change as soon as his mother entered the room. Perhaps he just wasn't ready for it. Meeting someone's mother on a second date is a bit intense. Or perhaps it's me. Maybe he was ashamed for me to meet her, when I'm so unlike them, and my life so unlike theirs.

I finish my starter as Andrew gets the main course ready. I notice he hasn't finished his, presumably put off by his mother's surprise appearance. Neither of us seems to know what to talk about, so while he plates up dinner, I sit and sip my wine, wondering how anyone copes with having a child while still a child themselves. At thirty-one, I still have days when I feel barely capable of looking after myself. By the time Rachel was my age, she had a son who was sitting his GCSEs.

'It must have been hard for her,' I say, as Andrew sets a mouth-watering plate of lamb shank and roasted vegetables in front of me. His cooking skills put mine to shame, and I wonder how disappointed he's going to be when it's my turn to host and he ends up with a pizza.

'For my mother?'

'Yeah. My God, this looks incredible. Did you train with Michel Roux?'

Andrew laughs. 'You haven't tasted it yet. And in answer to your question,' he says, setting his own plate at the other side of the table, 'yes. It wasn't easy for her. We lived with her grandmother for the first few years of my life, but she died when I was four. I don't really remember her. After that, we were on our own, just Mum and me. She did everything she could to be everyone to me – mother, father, grandparents. Earlier this year, she hit a bit of a bad patch. Relationship break-up. Letting her stay for a while was the least that I could do.'

'You don't need to justify it.'

There's a moment of uncomfortable silence in which neither of us seems to know what to say. Andrew obviously thinks I've made a judgement, and if I'm honest, at first, I did.

'Anyway,' he says, seeming keen to shift the conversation away from himself, 'what are you going to do about your landlord?'

I shrug. 'Stay out of his way as much as possible. And buy some earplugs.'

'You don't want to stay there now, do you? After this?'

'I don't have much choice. It's what I can afford.'

I'm grateful when Andrew doesn't pass comment. Despite his apparently humble upbringing, he's managed to make a success of his life. This house is evidence of that. I can't make any claim to the same. Where one door has closed, another has always been waiting just behind it, ready for a repeat slam in my face.

The conversation shifts to the restaurant where we'd been on our first date, and as we steer away from talk of his mother and my flat, the atmosphere seems to relax again. Andrew teases and flirts, and after dinner we move from the kitchen and take our drinks into the living room, where we sit together on the sofa, chatting and laughing until it's nearly midnight without either of us having noticed the passing of time.

'I'd better go,' I tell him. 'We've both got work tomorrow.'

'The bane of adult life.' He puts a hand to my hair and pushes it behind my ear. 'There's something about you, Daisy White.'

When he kisses me, I feel like I did outside the restaurant all over again: younger and carefree and weightless. His fingers cup my face as though he's handling something breakable, and as he pushes closer against me, my hands roam beneath his shirt to trace the contours of his stomach. I want to go upstairs with him and take off all his clothes, let him undress me, but I won't. Because if something's worth having, it's worth waiting for.

TEN

Andrew picks me up from the flat at six thirty, as we'd agreed.

'What do you fancy doing?' I ask, as I pull the seat belt across my chest. We didn't plan anything for this evening, though I'd assumed he may have had something in mind.

He eyes me and smiles teasingly. 'Do I answer that honestly or politely?'

'Whichever way you want.' The flirtation is catching, as though during his delivery of suggestive glances and loaded comments that has filled our last two encounters, he's been teaching me to reciprocate.

'I fancy getting to know you better,' he says as he turns the car from the end of my street. 'Shall we go somewhere quiet, where we can talk?'

Pontypridd isn't flush with quiet places during the daytime... in the evening, they're non-existent.

'We could always get a takeaway and eat it at yours?' I shoot him a look. What has happened to me?

'That sounds a perfect plan,' he says.

'I'm paying though,' I say. 'It was already agreed, so you can't break the promise.'

'I wouldn't dream of it,' he says with a smile.

I'm aware I've just invited myself over to his place, but if he has any issue with the suggestion, he doesn't voice it.

'I'm sorry I couldn't invite you into mine,' I tell him. 'I've got washing hanging everywhere... I haven't had a chance to tidy up.'

Andrew brushes off the apology. The truth is that I'm too embarrassed to let him see the flat, especially now I've seen his home.

As we make the drive from mine to his, he asks about my day, and I in turn ask about his. Talk of his job drifts over my head; in part because I have no clue what his job entails, but mostly because I'm distracted by the tone of his voice and just having him sitting here beside me, looking good enough to unwrap.

When we get to the house, there's music playing in the kitchen.

'Your mum's here?' I mouth, hesitating before I remove my shoes at the front door. It hadn't occurred to me to check whether she'd be home, and if she is, surely Andrew would have made an alternative suggestion. A takeaway for three sounds a bit too cosy and domesticated for a third date. Or any, for that matter.

He shakes his head. 'She's out with a friend tonight. I must have forgotten to turn off Alexa.'

I follow him down to the kitchen.

'Alexa,' Andrew says, 'recommend the best takeaways in Bridgend, please.'

'Impeccable manners with the virtual assistant,' I muse playfully. 'Such a gentleman.'

Andrew reaches for my waist and pulls me closer to him as Alexa reels off a short list of Chinese, Indian and Thai restaurants in the area. By the time he's finished kissing me, neither of us can remember what she's said, so he asks her to repeat the list.

'Which would you prefer?' he asks.

'Thai?'

'There's no wrong answer, Daisy,' he says with a laugh, as he opens the fridge and pulls out a bottle of wine. I feel as though I'm being mocked, but I'm not sure that's what he'd intended. He reaches for two wine glasses from a cupboard, and I notice the definition of his muscles beneath his sleeves.

He takes his phone from his pocket, unlocks it and searches for the Thai takeaway's website. 'Here,' he says, passing me his phone. 'Have a look at the menu, see what you fancy while I sort us some drinks.'

I sit at the dining table and scan the menu, not knowing what to choose. What is it with me? I seem to find it difficult to make a decision about even the smallest of things, while everything Andrew does and decides seems executed effortlessly.

He puts two glasses of wine on the table.

'Everything looks good,' I say, in a pathetic attempt to excuse my indecision.

When he takes the phone from me, our fingers graze. 'Is there anything you don't like?'

'Not really.'

He raises an eyebrow and glances at me suggestively before browsing the menu. 'How about I just order a few different things for us to share... a kind of gourmet lucky dip?'

'Sounds good.'

After he's selected what we'll eat and I've paid for the order, we go into the living room. The place is so tidy it's almost unnerving. I feel reluctant to sit down in case I disturb a scatter cushion, and I wonder whether the desire to have everything just-so comes from Andrew or from Rachel.

Andrew sits and pats the cushion beside him, and I sit down. He clinks his glass gently against mine.

'Cheers.'

'What are we toasting?' I ask.

'I don't know. Me finding you?'

His eyes stay fixed on me as he sips his drink. I do the same, and the alcohol seems to rush straight to my brain. Or maybe it's just lust.

He puts his drink on the table before taking my glass from me and putting it next to his. Our knees are touching.

'Tell me something about you, Daisy. Something I don't yet know.'

'I'm pretty boring,' I reply.

'I doubt that.' He reaches for my face, his fingertips tracing my jawline. 'Tell me something boring... tell me anything.'

His hand moves to the back of my neck, his fingers knotting in my hair.

'I'm a really bad singer.'

'How bad?'

His face is inches from mine, and my breath catches as his mouth takes the place of where his fingers just were, tracing the curve of my jaw.

'Keep talking,' he instructs me, but as his mouth moves to my throat, I can't concentrate on anything other than the thrill that has rushed through my limbs, raising my skin in goose-bumps. 'How bad?' he asks again.

'Paid to get off the karaoke bad,' I manage to say.

He laughs before his mouth finds mine, silencing us both. His tongue tastes like wine and his fingers feel like feathers as they move beneath my top and skit across my stomach. I follow his lead, my hands roaming beneath his shirt and finding the hard contours of his back as he pulls me closer to him. The thought that things are moving too fast passes quickly as he lifts my top over my head, but I don't want him to stop and so I let it happen, straddling him, my back arched as he kisses my collarbone.

And then the living door bursts open. I grab a cushion and cover myself hastily as Rachel stops abruptly in the doorway, seemingly unfazed by having walked in on us – her expression little more than a raised eyebrow. Neither Andrew nor I heard the front door.

'Oh,' she says casually. 'Sorry.' She doesn't look it. 'I didn't know you were home tonight.'

'And I didn't know *you* were,' Andrew replies coolly. 'I thought you were going out with a friend.'

I move quickly off him and press myself against the back of the sofa, so embarrassed I wish I could disappear into the cushions. One of my bra straps is hanging loose, so I slide it back up on to my shoulder.

'That's tomorrow. Anyway,' she says, letting her eyes rest on me for longer than feels comfortable, 'I won't disturb you any longer. It's nice to see you again, Daisy.'

Her smile sharpens, slicing a knife through her words. I grip the cushion closer to my chest, feeling as though she's somehow able to see through it. When she leaves the room, she closes the living room door behind her, and we wait a moment, hearing her footsteps on the stairs. Andrew can't look me in the eye.

'I'm so sorry,' he says.

'It's fine,' I lie. I pull my top on hastily, now self-conscious at having him see me half-dressed.

When he hands me my drink, he finally manages to look at me. 'Did you really get paid to get off a karaoke?'

I take the glass and nod before drinking more than is probably polite in one go, allowing the alcohol to hit me with an effect I hope will be quickly numbing.

'That's quite an achievement,' he jokes, but his words land flat. The moment has been killed, and we both know that whatever might have happened between us tonight has been taken off the menu. I'm grateful when the doorbell rings. The food will provide a distraction from what's just happened, and at least we'll have something to focus on other than Andrew's seemingly ever-present mother.

ELEVEN

Weeks pass, and the thought of another approaching Christmas starts to make me feel as it does every year: cold. I don't know what Christmas feels like to most people, that kind of warm, glow-inside sensation that's rammed down throats by advertising companies and marketing teams. But maybe that's just it. Maybe 'most' people don't feel this way at all – we're just manipulated to believe that everyone else is carrying the joy of relentless festivity around with them.

The store has got busier with every November weekend, and as we near the end of the month, I'm already sick of Mariah Carey's warbling falsetto, and just a waft of cinnamon is enough to make me heave. By the time my Sunday shift finishes, I can't wait to get home to a quiet night in, just me and the book that I've been trying – and failing – to read for the past month. There's been an obvious distraction to my focus, even when I've not been with him. For these past few weeks, Andrew has consumed my thoughts. I've daydreamed about him while I've been at work. I've fantasised about him while I've been in bed at night, unable to sleep. When we've been together – always out somewhere, and never at his place since his mother walked in on us – I have been completely and utterly enraptured by everything that he is and does. The man is a drug, and I have no desire to try to control my addiction.

Since the mugging, I make a point to always leave the store via one of the customer entrances. Whenever my shift ends after the store closes, I always make sure I'm leaving with someone else. Today, it's Claire, the department manager. She knows about the incident: with my face as it was, I couldn't really conceal the fact that I'd been attacked, and as I'm useless at lying, I was forced to admit what had happened at the back of the store. CCTV has since been put closer to the gate that leads out into the lane at the back of the building – locking the gate after the horse has bolted, as Aisha put it.

If Claire senses my unease, she doesn't mention it, but I notice that she stays with me until we're out on the bustle of the high street, and I'm grateful for it. Since the attack, I find myself walking home in the dark with my keys gripped between my fingers. I check the door and window locks three times before going to bed. The rational part of my brain reminds me that it was a random attack, and that the chances of anything like it ever happening again are now as minimal as they can be. But the memory of that fear that had gripped me in that moment is enough to shatter any attempt at rational thinking.

I manage to get a window seat on the train, and I sit with my face turned from the rest of the carriage, lost in thoughts of the train journey with Andrew on the day we'd met. Since going over to his house for dinner a few weeks ago, we've been on a further five dates, and with each one I've found myself more attracted to him. He is smart and funny and sexy as hell, and when I'm with him, I lose thoughts of everything and everyone else.

My phone pings in my bag. As if he'd known I was thinking about him, the message is from Andrew.

When can I see you this week? X

Whenever you want to, I type back. Since our first meeting, the relentless flirtation between us has ramped up with every text and every meeting. I haven't wanted to keep my hands off him, but as we've met up in public places for every date since Rachel sabotaged our third, I've been forced to exercise a self-restraint that's been almost painful.

Are you working Tuesday? I can take the afternoon off x

I'm supposed to be in work until 7 p.m. on Tuesday, but I'm sure Aisha won't mind covering a few hours for me if I take on some of hers the following weekend.

Let me see what I can do x

By the time I get back to the flat, my head has been filled with twenty different fantasies of how Andrew and I might spend Tuesday afternoon together: my favourite being the one where we don't leave his bedroom other than to refill our wine glasses and use the bathroom. There's only one problem with that idea: Rachel. I've no idea whether Andrew's mum works or not, though seeing as she's so young, I imagine she must. Either way, I don't fancy the chance of being caught in the act again. I could invite him over to the flat, but after seeing his house, I'm too embarrassed to invite him over. I also don't trust Craig not to listen in on us.

When I get through the front door, the noise of the television in the downstairs flat greets me in the hallway. I pick up the post that, as always, has been left on the carpet beneath the letter box, and I let myself into the flat, feeling the chill of the place hit me as I walk up the stairs. I swear it's warmer outside. When I get up on to the landing, something feels off. I don't know how else to describe it; there's just this sense of something being not quite right, like I left the flat in one way earlier and have come to find it another: some intangible, invisible shift that just sits in the air. I put it down to the after-effects of the mugging and shake it off as paranoia.

In the kitchen, I turn on the heating. I'll just blast it for an hour to take the edge off the chill, by which time I'll have made a nest of blankets on the sofa and will have warmed myself from the inside with a glass or two of wine – a much cheaper alternative to energy bills if you buy the right – or wrong – brand. I kick off my shoes and leave them on the landing, then I go to the bathroom and turn on the shower. I stay under the stream of hot water for longer than is necessary, not wanting to get back out into the cold. As I shower, I imagine that Andrew is here with me, his wet, naked body pressed against mine as he does unspeakable things to me. In my fantasy, the shower is not my own. We're not in this hell hole of a flat; instead, the shower is one of those huge walk-in types, the ones you get in the kind of fancy hotels I've never been able to afford to stay at and have only ever seen on TV. It's big enough to have sex in every position we can think of, and by the time I've finished working my way through every mental image, I must have been standing in my own shower for over twenty minutes. So much for saving on the energy bill, when the water meter will now be sky high.

When I get out from the shower and wrap myself in a towel, I am racked with guilt. It's the same pattern as always: I feel something that excites me, I linger on it... then I torture myself with guilt afterwards. The therapists I've seen in the past have all referred to it as survivor's guilt. For the past five years, everything I've done has been shadowed with the thought of what my brother's missing out on. Any new experience has been something that he will never have. Each possibility of a new relationship has been a potential for a happiness he will never now know. How can I carry on with my own existence, enjoying places and things and people, while he has been robbed of his life?

I fight back tears as I dry my hair, and once I'm done, I go into the bedroom to get a pair of pyjamas and some underwear. But before I reach the chest of drawers, I notice something is wrong. The top drawer – the drawer where I keep my underwear – is half-open. The sight of it stops me in my tracks, and I hang back near the doorway, as though someone might jump out from beneath the bed. I think back to this morning, when I was getting ready for work. I know I didn't leave the drawer open. I always close cupboards and drawers: in fact, it's something I do even when I'm in other people's houses. I'm the kind of person to straighten a photograph on someone else's living room wall, because things being out of line irrationally bothers me.

When I go to the drawer, I realise the things inside are also not as I left them. Bras to the left; knickers to the right. Call me obsessive, but I like things as I like them, where I know they'll be easily found. In a life that's been far from ordered, I suppose I like to maintain some semblance of control over the things I'm actually able to manage. And my personal belongings are those things. That's why I'd never leave a bra strewn across the top of everything else – and the bra that's been left like this is my most expensive item of underwear: one I haven't worn since my date at Andrew's house three weeks ago.

I dress quickly, throwing on a pair of knickers and some pyjamas. When I check the rest of the room – bed, wardrobe, bedside table – everything else seems to be in place. But I know without any doubt that someone has been in here; I can just feel it. And I should have listened to my senses when I'd first come up the stairs and on to the landing.

After going back through the living room and checking the kitchen and the bathroom – as though an intruder could have found anywhere to hide in this limited space – I get a glass of wine to settle my nerves and grab my phone, taking both with me to the sofa, where I call Aisha. She answers after just a couple of rings.

'Someone's been in the flat.'

'What do you mean? How?'

'Craig from downstairs. He's got a key, hasn't he? He's been snooping around in my things.'

'Whoa,' she says. 'Slow down a bit. How do you know this?'

I tell her what's happened since I arrived home from work, from feeling something 'off' on the landing, to finding my underwear rummaged through.

'You're definitely sure?'

'Aisha, you've known me long enough. Just think what I'm like at work.'

There have been plenty of times she's seen me follow behind other staff members, straightening clothes on racks or adjusting items on display so that they're all arranged at the same angle.

'Okay, good point. Urgh... what a fucking creep.' I don't think I've ever heard Aisha swear before. 'I still can't get that sweaty one-pack out of my head.'

'Oh God. Thanks for the reminder.'

'He's the only person with a spare key?'

'He is now. I had to take back my spare from the woman across the street after the mugging.'

Aisha falls silent for a moment. 'That does mean there's someone else who has a key though. Whoever took that bag.'

'I suppose so, in theory. But the kid who attacked me doesn't have a clue where I live, and he wouldn't care anyway – he probably dumped the bag when he emptied the money out of it. You've seen Craig for yourself now... he's creepy enough to sniff through someone's underwear.'

I stop talking. I've made myself feel sick.

'Eww.'

'You get my point though.'

'It's been weeks since the police came round,' Aisha says. 'Why would he do this now?'

'I don't know,' I admit. 'Maybe he's trying to unnerve me after what happened.'

'Get the lock changed.'

'I don't know that I can do that, can I? It's his flat.'

'Check online. See what the rules are. There's surely something legal saying he can't just let himself in without you knowing. Shouldn't he give you notice or something?'

'What, like he knocks on the door and tells me he'll be over in twenty-four hours to sift through my pants?'

I laugh, even though I feel like crying. My privacy has been invaded, and it feels violating.

'Do you want me to come and stay over tonight?' she offers. I love Aisha for this, and it's one of the reasons she's become my closest friend. But she already has enough to deal with and looking after me is a burden she can do without.

'No. But thank you. I appreciate the offer. It'll be fine.'

I ask her about her grandparents, and she tells me they're both doing okay. But I know from the polite but brief answers that 'okay' is probably far from that. I feel guilty for burdening her with my own problems when she has so many of her worries.

'When are you seeing Mr Perfume again then?'

It's only when she asks me that I remember Andrew's text from earlier.

'His name is Andrew,' I say with a smile. 'And he asked if we can meet this week. Which brings me to a question... what time are you working until on Tuesday?'

'Four. Why's that?'

'It's okay,' I tell her, changing my mind about asking. 'It doesn't matter.' I shouldn't be asking Aisha for favours; I can see Andrew another day.

'You need cover?' she asks. 'I don't mind.'

'Only until seven. I'll take some hours off you next weekend... call it a swap?'

'That might work out better for me anyway, if you don't mind. I might be going somewhere myself on Friday night...'

'Go on... the suspense is killing me.'

'Remember the guy I met at that festival last year?'

'The one who was off backpacking to find himself?'

'That's the one. Well, he's found himself... and he's back.'

An alarm bell sounds in my head. I can't remember the man's name, but I remember clearly the disappointment he'd left Aisha with when he'd stood her up last minute after several dates.

'You're meeting up with him again?' I say, stating the obvious while I try to disguise my reservations.

'Things were tricky for him before, what with going away and everything. But if I take your Tuesday hours and you could cover me a few for Friday afternoon, that would be perfect.'

'You're a star,' I tell her, withholding my thoughts on her date. 'I owe you.'

'Yeah, yeah. Just promise me one thing: if you're sure that pervy prick from downstairs has been in your flat, report him to the police.'

I make a promise that I will do, vowing at least to find out what the rules are about landlords letting themselves into rented property.

After our call ends, I text Andrew.

Can finish work at 4 on Tuesday if you're still up for meeting then? X

It's barely minutes before a reply comes through.

I'll come and meet you from work x

I don't ask him what he's got planned for us, because I know there'll be something he has in mind. The mystery is intriguing, and if I ask, there's a chance I'll spoil what might be intended as a surprise. Instead, we text back and forth for a while, until I momentarily forget all thoughts of my landlord being here in my bedroom.

It's later, when I'm taking my make-up off at the mirror in my bedroom, that I see a flash of red in the reflection of the glass. It's so small and brief that I question for a moment whether it was even there at all. But I know I didn't imagine it... I just don't know where it came from. I search the bedroom, standing on the bed to reach the top of the wardrobe, and running a finger around the picture rails, searching for something to prove I didn't imagine it. Because my mind has dragged me to a place I don't want to be taken – yet it makes sense in light of what I already know. Perhaps Craig didn't come in here to take something. Maybe he left something behind.

My stomach flips at the memory of the way he looked at me the night I went on my first date with Andrew. What if Craig has planted a camera somewhere? But half an hour later, my search of the flat has yielded nothing.

TWELVE

On Tuesday, Andrew meets me at the department store, as promised. I'd expected him to text me to let me know where he was waiting outside; instead, ten minutes before my shift is due to end, Aisha comes to find me to let me know he's here. She lets out a low whistle.

'How the hell have you two not done it yet?' she whispers, not quite quietly enough.

'His mother,' I quietly remind her.

Aisha stifles a snigger.

'Anyway,' I say, 'maybe it's for the best. Do you eat a whole chocolate cake at once?'

'If it looked like that I would. In one mouthful.'

We laugh, and I shush her as Andrew approaches. I mean, she's right though. He is gorgeous.

'This is my friend, Aisha,' I say, introducing them.

'Nice to meet you, Aisha. And thank you. I understand it's because of you I get to take Daisy out today?'

'Absolutely no hard feelings though... I obviously love spending more time in this place than I have to.' She rolls her eyes and tells us to enjoy ourselves before heading back to work.

'Give me five minutes,' I say to Andrew. 'I'll meet you down by the main doors.'

We spend the afternoon walking around Cardiff's Christmas markets, where we sample mulled wine and roasted chestnuts. As the afternoon fades to twilight and the temperature starts to drop, we stop at a small independent café that has blankets on their outdoor seating, and we drink cinnamon-spiced hot chocolate topped with marshmallows and cream as we watch shoppers and city workers pass the front of the castle's walls.

'I can't do this anymore,' I tell him.

'Can't do what?'

'These dates.'

Disappointment floods Andrew's face for a moment before he quickly straightens himself in his chair, his features resting into a seemingly forced nonchalance. My heart stutters at the thought that maybe this is more to him than just a bit of fun. His reaction certainly suggests so.

'Okay,' is all he says, politely accepting of my apparent rejection.

'I'll be two hundred pounds by Christmas.'

His mouth widens in a smile. 'I'll take you for a run next time,' he suggests. 'Problem solved.'

'Urgh... it's too cold for that. Potentially icy... far too dangerous.'

He leans over to me and reaches for my chin, tilting my face up towards his as he lowers his mouth over mine. He tastes of chocolate, and I stifle a laugh as I think of Aisha's earlier comment about eating the cake in one mouthful.

'What?' he asks, sensing that something has humoured me.

'Nothing.' I kiss him again, wishing we were somewhere else, somewhere more private. He's never tried to push for it, and I wonder whether he's just being polite or if there's something wrong with me that's holding him back.

'Let me drive you home,' he says, as we leave the café an hour later. 'The trains are a nightmare.'

My place seems a squat compared to his house, and I haven't told him about what happened on Sunday either. If I tell Andrew that I think Craig was in there, he might confront him about it if we happen to bump into him, and the last thing I need is anything else to disgruntle my already unhappy landlord.

'Look,' he says. 'I haven't been entirely honest with you.'

I feel a creeping sense of unease. 'What do you mean? What is it?'

'Nothing bad,' he says with a smile, seeing the panic that must have spread across my face.

'I just needed an excuse to get the car here. I've got something for you in the boot.'

Intrigued, I get out from the car when he does, and follow him to the back, where he opens the boot. He lifts out something large, flat and rectangular wrapped in shiny gold paper – the same kind of paper I'd used to wrap the perfume he'd bought for his mother on the day we met.

'What is it?'

'If I tell you that, there'd have been no point in wrapping it, would there? Can I carry it in for you?'

I hesitate on a 'no', but I don't want to appear standoffish. What's the worst that could happen? If things between Andrew and me continue to go as well as they are, he's going to have to come up to the flat at some point.

'Okay. Thank you.'

He follows me into the communal hallway, where the sound of Craig's television greets us with a burst of gunfire and screams as we step through the front door. I register the look on Andrew's face as he remembers my anecdote about the evening Aisha called the police after hearing a scream from downstairs.

'Best not to ask?'

I pull a face as I unlock the door to my flat. 'Come on up,' I tell him. 'Just please ignore the state of the place.'

He follows me upstairs, where the first of the flat's many damp patches greets us on the landing. 'Would you like a cup of tea or something? Coffee?'

'Tea would be great, if you're sure I'm not keeping you?'

I cast him a look. I would keep him here forever if I could, if we were able to just shut ourselves away and forget about our jobs and our commitments.

I go into the kitchen and flick on the kettle. Andrew stands in the doorway, and I sense him taking in the details of the small room and my minimalist life. If he has any thoughts on either, he keeps them to himself. I make tea for us both and he follows me into the living room, where he carefully props the package against the sofa. Yet another patch of damp stains the wall behind it. I'd meant to redecorate, but it's something I've just not yet managed to get around to.

'Thanks,' he says, taking one of the cups I've placed on the coffee table. 'Please don't keep me in suspense much longer.'

He gestures to the package. Whatever this thing is, he clearly can't wait for me to look at it. I sit at the end of the sofa and gently prise the Sellotape from the corner of the package, not wanting to tear through the pretty paper and the effort that's apparently gone into wrapping it. A memory of our conversation at the department store that day is reignited, when Andrew had commented on how his mother would know the perfume hadn't been wrapped by him, and I wonder now whether she did this for him. The idea of it halts my progress for a second, before my fingertips meet with the hardness of wood, and when I tear lengthways along the edge of the paper, I'm met with the brown backing of a frame.

'This is really kind of you,' I tell him, 'but it's not even Christmas yet.'

He says nothing, watching me expectantly.

I turn the frame. And I can't believe what I find myself looking at. A man and a woman running across a road at the end of a row of terraced houses, on a street that looks very much like the one on which I'd spent my childhood.

'The painting from the restaurant,' I say quietly, unable to tear my eyes from it. It is beautiful, and this is one of the loveliest things anyone has ever done for me.

'Yes. I mean, not the same one, obviously, but a print of the same painting. It's called *Running Away with the Hairdresser*.'

There is silence as I study the image, gripping the frame with both hands as I try not to react to the thoughtfulness of the gift.

'Please don't feel obligated to put it up anywhere. Sorry... perhaps it was too much.'

'No,' I say quickly. 'It's lovely. Really.' Perfect, I think. Just like him. 'Thank you. I can't wait to get it up on the wall.'

'Do you have a drill?'

'Do I look like someone who owns a drill? I wouldn't know what to do with it.'

Andrew grins, and his eyes seem to sparkle. 'I'm sure you would,' he says, sitting next to me on the sofa so that our hips are touching. 'It would be in very capable hands.'

Things get heated very, very quickly. He pushes me back on to the sofa, pinning one of my wrists above my head while my free hand works to undo his belt. His other hand moves beneath my sweater and slides up my back, where he does an impressive job of removing my bra with one deft movement.

'My God, you're so sexy,' he whispers in my ear, and I feel the last of my resolve melt as my hand closes around him.

Things might be moving quickly, but I have never wanted anything or anyone as much as I want Andrew.

And then I think of Craig in the flat downstairs. The flash of a red light in the mirror. I remember the possibility of a hidden camera that I may not have been clever enough to find.

'I'm sorry, I can't do this here.'

With my words, Andrew backs straight off me, pushing himself up on to his knees. He looks as though I've just slapped him across the face. 'Have I done something wrong?'

'No! It's not you. Oh God... I didn't mean it like that.' I sit up and adjust my top, conscious that my bra is hanging half-off. 'There's something I haven't told you. On Sunday... I think the landlord was in my flat.'

'What?'

I explain to him what happened, relating the same story to him as I did to Aisha. Then I admit that I couldn't sleep on Sunday night for the thought that Craig might have hidden a camera somewhere to spy on me.

'I've checked everywhere since then,' I tell him, 'and I've found nothing. But you can see why I don't want to do this here... just in case.'

Andrew's face has changed. The beautiful bronze eyes have darkened, and his jaw has tightened. 'You need to report him to the police. He might own the place, but he can't just come in here without your consent.'

He gets up from the sofa.

'Where are you going?'

'To pay your landlord a visit.'

'Andrew,' I say, getting up to follow him. 'Please don't. I know you mean well, but you'll only make things more difficult for me.' I grab his arm when he gets to the hallway. 'Please. I'll deal with it.'

'How?' His eyebrow arches. He knows it's just something to say to stop him from going down there. 'Daisy, you deserve better than this. The place is riddled with damp, and those curtains hiding that leak above the window aren't going to make it go away. It's a fucking disgrace that he's letting you live like this.'

'I'll sort it out. I'll speak to him again about the damp.'

'And the fact that he was in here on Sunday?'

'I'll report him to the police.'

He puts his hands on my shoulders. 'I could help you find another flat.'

'Trust me, I've been keeping an eye out for one for ages. But there's nothing this close to Cardiff anywhere near what I pay for this. I'd end up on a mountain somewhere. This is far enough away from work as it is.'

'Do you want to stay at mine tonight? Nothing like that... there's a spare room.'

'Thank you, but I'll be fine. He can't get in here while I'm home – there's a deadlock on the door.'

Andrew looks to the floor and exhales loudly. 'Let me stay over. I'll take the sofa... I just don't like the idea of you being here on your own, not after what you've told me.'

'I'm fine,' I say firmly, not wanting this fuss. I wish now that I hadn't mentioned it. 'Please... I'm just tired.'

He looks as though he's going to argue with me about it, but then thinks better of it. 'If you need me for anything, just call, okay?'

'Okay. And thank you for the print. It's beautiful.'

He kisses me and I go downstairs to see him leave. But at the door to the flat, he makes me go inside and put the deadbolt on before he goes. Within moments of him leaving, I get a text.

You don't have to live like this, Daisy. See you soon x

I go to the bedroom window and watch his car pull away from the kerb. The day plays back like a film reel in my head, and I'm filled with a rush of warmth that's so intense it might keep me from needing to put the heating on for the rest of winter. Yet when I go back into the living room and see the damp patches on the wall and the leak above the window, I hear Andrew's words repeat in my head, and for the first time ever, I might believe them to be true. Perhaps I do deserve better than this.

THIRTEEN

Outside Liam's bedroom, the treetops are iced with frost. It's another picture-perfect Christmas scene, much like the robin we saw there during my last visit. It seems ironic when I look back inside the room at the hospital-style bed and paraphernalia that are essential for Liam's condition. No matter the attempts to make the place feel like some kind of home, it never will be.

Since he told me that afternoon to go home, we haven't spoken about what happened. I don't want to linger on it, and I know his mood will be different today. I could never hold a grudge with Liam. He's angry, and I understand it. Not completely, of course – that would be impossible for anyone. But the last thing I want to do is invalidate his feelings, whatever they might be towards me.

Despite the wealth of paperwork and literature I was given after Liam's diagnosis, I don't think even the most proficient of brain specialists could ever know the extent of the injuries Liam sustained. No number of scans could ever reveal the impact on Liam's emotional state, and his fluctuating moods remain for the most a mystery. White-coated professionals can see the medical facts of the condition, but the true effects of the syndrome which has stolen Liam from me remain for now with him, though I hope one day to be able to unlock his full potential to share his experiences with me.

After the accident in Ibiza, Liam was airlifted to Son Dureta hospital in Palma, Majorca, where he spent six weeks in a medical coma, having suffered an anoxic brain injury. He'd been submerged in the water for twelve minutes by the time he was freed by the rescue services, by which point his brain had been starved of oxygen for long enough that the damage was irreversible. Those weeks that followed were the longest and most torturous of my life, not knowing when or whether he would wake up, with no idea of the extent to which his brain might have been affected. It was a miracle that he was still alive. I was reminded frequently of the fact by various members of the medical team who treated him, though during those weeks that Liam lay inert and unresponsive, I couldn't help but wonder whether the life he might wake up to would be worth him holding on for.

'It always seems to come around so quickly, doesn't it,' I say. 'Christmas.'

Today, the silence is crushing.

'Would you like to talk today?'

Two blinks in quick succession. No.

I bite my lip.

'I'm doing my best,' I tell him. 'I know it's not always good enough. I know I should have done better in the past. But I'm doing what I can now, and I know you hate me, and believe me, I hate myself just as much. But God knows I'm trying, Liam.'

'Cup of tea, love?'

My head snaps to the doorway as one of the staff appears with a drinks trolley. I wonder how much of my outburst she just overheard. They seem to like me here; they show me sympathy and compassion, all the while ignorant of the fact that I am so undeserving of either of these things.

'Yes, please.'

She doesn't ask whether I take milk or sugar; she's seen me so many times now that she manages to remember how I drink my tea.

'Afternoon, Liam,' she says, as she comes into the room and puts my tea on the bedside table. 'How are we feeling today?'

She puts a hand on his shoulder and rubs it affectionately. How easily it seems to come to them, this ability to be so patient and so kind, even when there is nothing to be reciprocated from their efforts. Yet that's the point... it is effortless for them. She must consider me with disdain now, having heard me speak so unkindly to someone who isn't able to offer a response. I wonder what is said about me when I'm not here.

'You started getting ready for Christmas yet?' she asks me, as she pulls up the blinds to allow more winter sunshine to spill into the room.

'Not really. I probably should though.'

'I love this time of year,' she says to no one in particular. 'We might even get a white Christmas for once, the way the temperatures are going.'

The weather, I think. Everything always comes back to the weather. Or to tea. Two subjects on which the British can be relied to fall back upon in times of a conversation drought or a crisis deemed irreparable.

'What about you?' I ask, although I don't really want to hear her plans. Other people's festive family joy cuts deep these days. No one pays much thought to the people who don't have relatives to open presents with or read bad jokes out of crackers to.

'Few bits and bobs left. I like to be organised. I'm working Christmas Day this year though, Liam. You're stuck with me,

I'm afraid. We can watch the King's speech together, what do you think?'

I'm tempted to point out that Liam would probably rather offer up his own severed fingers as the pigs in blankets than be subjected to sitting through a Christmas Day royal speech, but as she's only making conversation and she's obviously trying to be nice, I hold back the urge and keep the words to myself.

'Let me know if you need anything else.'

I wait to hear her go into the next room, chattering away pleasantly to someone else who can't respond to her enthusiasm. Once she's gone, Liam's room falls into a painful silence. I can usually find something to talk about. Before now, I've filled whole hours with talk of goodness-knows-what, somehow managing to steer clear of the things that might cause him unnecessary suffering. I avoid talk of work. I stay away from the subject of friends. I've considered talking to him about Andrew, but it doesn't feel right. That part of my life is separate from Liam, my love life something he's never been involved with. It always feels so wrong to talk about the 'normal' everyday things he's been so brutally removed from. Besides anything else, I don't want him to worry about what's going on outside this place. Perhaps it's the case that the less he knows about my life, the better for us both.

I get up and close the bedroom door before going to the drawer where Liam's notebooks and letter boards are kept. Although he can't turn his head, I can sense his eyes following me, feeling the heat of his attentive gaze upon my back. I open the drawer, and with my back to him, I rifle through the notebooks where his communications are stored. I look for a mention of my name, wondering whether he's been talking about me with any of the staff here, but there is nothing. No hint of how he feels towards me. No suggestion of what he knows.

I'm not sure whether to feel upset or relieved at the fact that he hasn't been talking about me.

I was telling the truth when I told him I'm sorry, but I've known for a long time now that words are no longer enough. They never have been, and if I spoke from now until the end of time, they still wouldn't begin to fill the gaps I created a long time ago. If I want Liam to start believing in my remorse, I'm going to need to show him just how sorry I truly am.

FOURTEEN

That evening, I'm about to get in the bath when Andrew calls.

'Hey,' he says. 'You busy?'

'I've got a date with some bubbles and a book.'

'Ahh. Too busy for company then?'

I go through the living room and into the bedroom. At the window, I see him in his car. 'Are you stalking me?'

'Do you want to be stalked?'

He looks up at the flat and smiles when he sees me standing here, and the bath suddenly seems less appealing than it did just moments ago.

'I'll be down in a minute.'

I close the curtains before taking off my dressing gown and putting on some leggings and a T-shirt.

When I get downstairs, Andrew is waiting at the front door. He's carrying a black box.

'I've got a drill,' he announces, 'and I'm not afraid to use it.'

I laugh and step aside to let him into the house. I notice him cast a disapproving glance at the door to Craig's flat before following me up the stairs to my own. The landing smells of sandalwood and patchouli – a birthday treat from Aisha that I've been saving for a special occasion. The only thing that had made tonight 'special' was the realisation I'd never get around to ever using the bath soak if I kept waiting for the 'right' time.

'When you said bubbles, I assumed you meant Prosecco,' Andrew says, as we go into the living room.

I pull a face. 'Who drinks Prosecco on their own at home?'

As I ask the question, I wonder if Rachel does. I picture her sitting on the plush sofa in Andrew's living room, sipping from a champagne flute while wearing a silk dressing gown and flicking through a glossy magazine, delicately licking the tip of a perfectly manicured finger every time she turns a page. The image is so ludicrously over the top that it makes me smile. Thankfully, Andrew doesn't catch it.

'Were you just about to get in the bath?' he asks.

'It doesn't matter.'

'Yes, it does. I should have called before just turning up. I'm sorry.'

'It's honestly fine. Do you want a cup of tea or something?'

'That'd be lovely.'

He leaves the drill box by the sofa, where the print he bought me is still propped. In the kitchen, I ask him about his day while I make us both tea and it turns out that data security really is as boring as it sounds.

'Let me set the drill up while you do this,' he says, and I finish making the teas while he's in the living room.

'Any thoughts on where you'd like this?' he asks, gesturing to the print.

I put our mugs on the coffee table. 'I was thinking over here.' I move to the internal wall that separates the house from the one next door. 'About there. What do you think?'

He tilts his head, as though trying to visualise what the print would look like behind the sofa. I've probably been influenced by the one he's got in the same place in his own living room, although I wouldn't want to admit that to him.

'The only problem there is the window.'

'What do you mean?'

'At certain times of day, you're going to get the light streaming in through there, and it's going to hit the print. Especially during the summer. What about here?' he says, moving to the wall that divides the living room from the landing. 'It'll look really nice there... break up all that blank space.'

'Okay. Thank you.'

He takes his tea from the coffee table. 'I've got a confession,' he says, gesturing to the drill. 'It was just an excuse to see you.'

'You never need to make an excuse.'

'I've got an idea. Why don't you have your bath while I get this print up? Have you eaten? I could order us a takeaway.'

'Don't worry about the bath.'

'You've run it now. It'd be a shame to waste all that water. Do it for the environment.'

I laugh. 'Okay. But I won't be long.'

I go into the bedroom and retrieve my towel and some clean clothes, not wanting to have to walk back out here undressed when I'm finished. It feels strange getting into the bath with Andrew in the other room, humming to himself while he sets about his task. Oddly domesticated. Nice, in a way that is so alienly normal.

I shampoo my hair quickly, not wanting to be in here for too long. I rinse it through with the shower before applying conditioner, and I'm about to sink back into the bubbles when I hear something like a crack from one of the other rooms. Andrew swears.

And then I hear what sounds disconcertingly like the hiss of water.

I get out of the bath quickly, my hair still full of conditioner.

With a towel wrapped around me and my skin still wet, I rush back through to the living room, where water is gushing through a hole in the wall, spraying in jets across the carpet.

'Oh, shit.'

'Where's the stopcock?' he asks.

I have no idea. I've never needed to use it... I'm not sure I'd even know what it looks like. Andrew drops the drill and heads past me. I stare in dismay at the plasterboard, which has cracked in a line that runs two thirds the length of the wall. There is water gushing everywhere.

In the kitchen, I find Andrew checking the cupboards.

'Got it.' He reappears from beneath the sink. 'Shit. I am so, so sorry.'

My first thought is Craig. I've already made myself unpopular enough with him, when Aisha and I invited the police over to what should have remained a strictly one-to-one event. This could be the final straw where my tenancy's concerned.

Andrew goes back into the living room, and I follow, remaining conscious of the fact that I'm still in a towel.

'Why is there still water coming out if you've turned off the stopcock?' I ask.

'It'll drain whatever's left in the pipes first.'

I feel sorry for him. He looks so embarrassed by what's happened.

'It's not your fault,' I try to reassure him.

'Of course it's my fault. I've just drilled through a pipe. I only hope it's not a mains.'

'Why?' I ask, feeling my heart sink. 'What will that mean?'

'Even worse damage.'

With my hair still clogged with conditioner, I go to get dressed. When I come back, Andrew's heading for the stairs.

'Where are you going?' I can't believe he's about to leave while the flat is in this mess. It may have been an accident, but he's surely not just going to leave me like this.

'To see the landlord. I'll explain it was my fault.'

'No,' I say, reaching for his arm to stop him. 'It's fine. Please. Let me sort it.'

'It was my mistake,' he says, ignoring my request. 'I'll deal with it.'

I wait at the top of the stairs, not knowing what to do. The last thing I want is to see Craig; I've successfully managed to avoid him since the night Aisha called the police, and I still think he was here in my flat. But I suppose I'll have to see him at some point, and with Andrew here is better than alone.

I hear his voice, smoke damaged and hostile, and moments later, he appears at the doorway at the foot of the staircase. 'D'you want to show me then, or what.'

Andrew reappears to lead him up to the flat. He reaches for my hand as he passes, squeezing my fingers gently, passing the unspoken message that everything is going to be okay. But I don't see how it can be. The flat was already barely habitable.

'What the fuck,' Craig exclaims as he enters the living room and sees the damage done. 'How the fuck did you manage that?'

'I already just told you,' Andrew says coolly.

'What are you, some sort of moron?'

I expect Andrew to react, but he doesn't. Instead, he remains calm and unflinching. 'I'll pay for the repairs.'

'You're fucking right you will. And you want to hope nothing leaks down to my place, or you'll be paying for that as well.' He turns and leaves, offering a few more expletives as a parting gesture.

'You didn't need to do that,' I tell him, once I've heard the door to Craig's flat close.

'You're not going to be able to stay here tonight. There's no water, the damp is even worse... you won't have any heating.'

'I don't have anywhere else to go. It'll be fine... I'll just wrap up warm and call a plumber in the morning.'

Andrew sits on the sofa and puts his head in his hands. 'I

was trying to do something nice for you. I can't believe the chaos it's caused.'

I sit next to him. Inwardly, I want to cry. God knows how much the repairs for this are going to cost, and I can't let him foot the bill. But I don't want him to see how worried I am about it, not when he already feels guilty enough.

We sit silently for a while, both assessing the extent of the damage.

'Come and stay at mine for tonight. I won't get under your feet – I just don't want you having to pay out to stay somewhere else while this mess gets fixed.'

'I'll manage here. I've got everything I need. I mean, I could have done with getting the conditioner out of my hair while the water was still warm, but worse things have happened. Plus, it's Rachel's home too... I can't just turn up unexpected.'

'You won't have any heating,' he reminds me again. 'I can't leave you in this mess, and we won't be able to get anyone out this late. My mother won't mind.'

I doubt that very much. And besides, I would mind... but I can't tell Andrew that.

'It's one night. It'll be fine.' I lean into him and kiss him on the mouth, forgetting at once how cold the flat has quickly become.

'I'm not leaving you alone here again,' he says. He slides a hand under my T-shirt, his fingers insistent. My stomach pimples with goosebumps at his touch. 'I promise to keep you warm.'

'Well,' I say, as my lips find his again, 'you know it's wrong to break a promise, don't you?'

His tongue fills my mouth, silencing my words. He peels off my clothes before removing his own, and it is everything I'd imagined it would be, only a million times better, and when we're done, and my heart and lungs are fit to burst, we move into the bedroom, where we lie together beneath the duvet and talk about the future. The chaos of the burst pipe is forgotten... the camera that may or may not exist becomes a distant memory... and in the absence of everything else, I realise that despite everything, I have never been this happy.

FIFTEEN

His foot is trapped beneath something. Amid the debris and the dust, I can't be sure what it is, but I think it's one of the beams from the ceiling. He is screaming in pain, crying out for someone to help us.

'Come on,' I tell him, as though he'll be able to free himself easily with mere instruction. 'We've got to get out of here.'

The water is cascading around us, now calf high when I stand. But he is on the floor of the boat, trapped by a fallen beam.

'You need to sit up,' I tell him. 'Can you sit up?'

I lift beneath his arms, heaving as I pull his weight upright. His right leg is pinned, but he uses the left to push himself up to a seated position. It gives us more time to try to get help, because I'm not going to be able to get him out of this on my own.

I try to push the beam, but when I do, he screams again.
'Daisy! Daisy!'
I can't leave him here, I think. I won't leave him here.
But the water is rising, and we are going to drown here.
'Daisy! Daisy, it's okay.'

My eyes snap open to find Andrew looking down at me. He is propped on an elbow, his hand on my shoulder, shaking me from my sleep. Lifting me out of my nightmare.

'You're okay,' he tells me, lowering himself next to me and pulling me into him. 'It was just a dream. Everything's okay.'

My heart is racing, and my palms are damp. I swear I'm still able to feel the cold steel of the ship's beam against my desperate hands.

'Do you want to talk about it?' he asks.

I shake my head, and that's enough for him to leave it. He doesn't ask again, and I'm grateful for it. As I leave the dream and return to the here and now, I'm reminded of the mess that awaits us at the other side of the bedroom door. I need to call a plumber, although God knows how long it'll take for one to come out. We're only a month from Christmas, and with the weather as cold as it's been, they're likely to be inundated with work.

'Thank you for staying last night.'

'I couldn't exactly leave you in this mess. Do you want me to call a plumber?'

He gets up from bed, still naked. I can't help but stare as he goes into the living room, returning with the clothes that were left there last night. He pulls his phone from the pocket of his jeans and checks the time.

'Do you know anyone?'

He shakes his head. 'We're going to have to trust Google.'

I move to the edge of the bed with the duvet held up over me, feeling self-conscious despite Andrew having now seen every part of me. I lean to the drawers and pull out some clothes while he searches for a local plumber. With the plasterboard needing replacing, along with plastering and a new carpet, it could cost thousands of pounds to put right. I would feel guilty accepting it, despite Andrew having caused the damage.

Now dressed, I sit on the edge of the bed and try to push the memory of my nightmare away from the front of my mind. Recently, the dreams have haunted me more often, returning like a curse I thought I'd managed to free myself from. After everything else, what happened that day was a cruelty of fate no one could have anticipated. If only we hadn't booked that boat party. If only we hadn't gone on that holiday.

But we had. We'd longed for escape and youth and total abandonment from everything our lives had thrown at us up until then. We had believed ourselves deserving of a break from the banality of our everyday existence, and we had paid the price for our search for hedonism.

That summer, we'd vowed to put all our previous troubles behind us, and God knows, there had been enough of them. After our mother had died when I was five and my brother was just three years old, our father had appeared to the outside world to cope as well as anyone could expect him to under circumstances for which he was pitied by family and friends. I knew, even at such a young age, that he hated the sympathy my mother's death had forced upon him: the expressions on the faces of people who would have rather looked away... the clichéd words of condolence that were intended to offer comfort. On the surface, our father seemed to get on with things, which in his own way, he did. He got us dressed in the mornings and to school on time: we were fed and loved and safe. But on the inside, when no one else was looking, he was silently falling to pieces.

He worked on the trains, as a technician. The company was supportive, with his bosses offering more time off than might have been 'policy'; I knew all this because he told me afterwards, years later when I was a teenager full of questions and a simmering resentment that for a while made me dislike the world and most of the people in it. But I never felt that way towards my father. Even amid the sporadic drink binges and the bouts of detachment that would see him distance himself from my brother and me for sometimes weeks at a time, my resentment never directed itself at him. I held on to the hope that one day, we would wake up and things would be different – that he might rise from the fog of grief that had kept him enveloped in a world nobody else could infiltrate, and we would come to live a different life. He would never forget my mother, but one day, perhaps, he would be able to move on from the life he'd lived with her.

But that day never came. Instead, one afternoon, while I was sitting in a Geography lesson wondering whether I'd made a mistake in choosing the subject for GCSE, the head teacher came to the doorway, and as soon as he spoke my name to call me from the classroom, I knew. I went into the corridor and followed him to his office, knowing that his silence was speaking far more words than any conversation could. When we got to the office, the deputy head teacher was also there. She was young for a deputy head, maybe late thirties, and she had a daughter who was in year seven and another at the local primary. I remember her standing near the desk, trying not to look as though she was about to burst into tears, and in those minutes that followed, all I recall is feeling sorry for her, that she was being made to endure the unenviable task of having to tell a child who had no mother that her father was now also dead.

A heart attack, they said. He was forty-seven.

At least you've still got the house. That was what someone had said to me, as though a pile of bricks could have softened the blow of losing our only remaining relative. There were no aunties or uncles, no grandparents to pick up where our father had unwittingly left off. There was no house either, as it turned out. Our father had got himself into so much debt after our mother had died that the house was repossessed. I was nearly sixteen: where social services were concerned, I wasn't a priority. But for three years, my brother lived in a foster home. I made a promise to him, that when he was sixteen and able to leave, we would live together. And we did. We lived together, found jobs together; we tried our best to make something of what was left behind. And we worked hard. We saved. Then that summer, when he was twenty-three and I was twenty-six, we decided to do something we'd never been able to do before: to be young and carefree. We booked a holiday to Ibiza with some of the money we'd saved, and that was the beginning of the end.

'Daisy.' Andrew's voice floats across the bedroom to me, as though from a dream. 'Did you hear what I said?'

I realise that, for these last few minutes, I've been here in body but not in mind.

'I just got hold of someone who says he can be here by lunchtime. I think that's the best we're going to get. Let me take you out for breakfast? He's got my number – he can call if he gets here before we're back.'

'Okay,' I say, without the energy to object.

But if feels wrong to be accepting his kindnesses so easily, when there's still so much that he doesn't know about me.

SIXTEEN

We eat breakfast in a café on the middle of the high street in town: poached eggs on toast and caramel lattes that warm us up ready to go back out into the cold. With time still to kill before the plumber is due to arrive, we stroll around the park that runs parallel with the river. In the playground, the swings hang still and the air rests quiet with an absence of children. The lido is shut up for winter, and the park has an almost eerie atmosphere to it, as though everything has frozen in preparation for a winter that seems to have started early this year.

We head towards a mini market, where I buy bottled water – some for drinking, the rest to wash my hair over the sink with when we get back. It's so matted from the unwashed-out conditioner of last night that I've had to scrape it back into a tangled bird's nest. Goodness knows what I look like this morning, but I reassure myself with the thought that Andrew has hung about, so it can't be all that bad.

'We'd better head back,' he says, checking his phone as we leave the shop. It's only now that I realise that he's made no mention of work today.

'Am I going to make you late for work?'

He takes me by the hand, his fingers icy with the cold air of the morning.

'I've got the morning off, it's fine.'

We head back to the flat, where we wait another hour and a half for the plumber to arrive. When he does, he cuts a large hole into the wall to assess the damage. One look leads to a series of hmmms and ahhhs. There's chin rubbing to follow.

'What is it?'

'You've gone through the mains pipe,' he tells me. 'Whole wall's going to have to come down. That was quite a direct hit, fair play. One hundred and eiiiighty.' He laughs at his own joke, but falls silent when he realises no one else has joined in.

I sense Andrew about to confess to the damage, so I quickly interrupt him. He already feels bad enough about what's happened.

'I'll lay off the DIY in future,' I say.

'Yeah, might be best.'

'Anyway... how long do you reckon it's going to take to fix?'

The man purses his lips and exhales as though he's blowing out smoke. 'Take the wall off... replace the pipe, put up some new plasterboard... have it all skimmed and decorated. I'm not going to be able to start for a few days either... this is all going to have to dry out. Have you got a dehumidifier?'

I shake my head. There's more chin rubbing.

'You own the place?'

'No. The landlord lives downstairs.'

'Might be worth me checking out down there. You never know, the damage might have run down into his place.'

Oh, great.

'I'll go,' Andrew volunteers, and before I can stop him, he's heading down the stairs to knock on Craig's door.

'The problem is,' the plumber continues, and I feel my stomach plummet a little further, 'you've got a fair few electrics going on in there. You're going to need someone to check that out... could be dangerous. And any new plasterboard will take a few days to dry out before it can be skimmed. I know a bloke who does that. Good lad... I can give you his number, if you like.'

'Thanks,' I say glumly. 'I'll be able to live here while the work's being done though?'

He pulls a face. 'If you can manage without water and heating, should be fine, yeah.'

We're interrupted by shouting. I go on to the landing to find Craig nearly at the top of the stairs, with Andrew just behind him. He shoots me a look that I'm not quite able to read.

'There's water run down my fucking wall,' he announces.

'Good morning, Craig,' I say blankly.

He narrows his eyes. 'Why'd you call him out?' He gestures to the plumber. 'You want work done, you go through me. I own the bloody place – I decide who comes in here.'

Don't I know it, I think.

'Listen, mate,' the plumber says, raising both hands as though Craig has just pulled out a gun from the waistband of his saggy pyjama bottoms, 'I just responded to the call-out.'

'Yeah, well, I've got my own plumber, so you're not needed.'

The man mumbles something that sounds like having his fucking time wasted, before grabbing his toolkit and leaving. Craig opens his greasy little mouth, a full-blown tirade imminent.

'If you think—'

But he doesn't get a chance to continue, because Andrew cuts him dead.

'Have you been in this flat while Daisy's been out?'

Craig turns on him, squaring up the pasty chest that ripples beneath his stained hoodie.

'What?'

'Have you,' Andrew repeats, slowing his words as though

he's talking to a small child. 'Been in. This flat. While Daisy has been out? It's a simple question. A yes or no answer will do.'

The colour rises in Craig's cottage-cheese cheeks. 'It's my flat. I can do what I like.'

'The police might think otherwise,' Andrew states.

Craig looks like he might spontaneously combust. Or punch someone. Despite his size, he's a good five inches shorter than Andrew, and I doubt he has much in the way of agility. It's more likely that he's tempted to hit me than Andrew.

'We know you've been in here,' he claims, with continuing calmness. 'And we have evidence to prove the fact. So unless you want to be facing charges for unlawful entry and harassment, I suggest you go back downstairs and contact the plumber you rate more highly than the one we already had here. What do you think?'

Craig glares at me. 'You're an ungrateful bitch,' he snaps. 'I could have put the rent up ages ago, but I didn't, and this is the thanks I get.'

He turns for the door but doesn't get a chance to make it there. Because Andrew punches him straight in the face. I watch open-mouthed as Craig's nose bursts in a splatter of red. His hands clasp his face, blood oozing between his fingers as he tries to stem the flow. He paints the air red with every expletive his vocabulary can conjure, and then he turns to me, his anger fired in a spray of spittle and blood.

'You're going to fucking pay for this!'

He staggers to the door, still swearing, and Andrew and I stand in silence until we hear his flat door close behind him. Craig's blood stains Andrew's knuckles.

'I can't believe you just did that,' I say quietly.

'He's got no right to speak to you like that.'

But I don't think he realises what he's done. This is my home. It may be a shithole, but it's been mine for the past nearly five years, and I've nowhere else to go. He's made it impossible for me to stay here now, whether I wanted to or not.

'I don't need you to fight my battles,' I snap, anger bursting from me. 'What the hell, Andrew – you can't just go around punching everyone who speaks to you in a way you don't like. You've just made everything ten times harder for me.'

'I was trying to protect you.'

'I'm thirty-one-years old, for Christ's sake. I've managed for this long without being protected – I don't need you stepping in and fucking everything up!'

We fall into silence, both of us taken aback at my words. I don't know what to think, and for now, I've nothing more to say to him. I just want him to leave, and I tell him so.

'Are you always this stubborn?' he asks.

'Are you always that violent?'

He looks crushed by my words, and by the insinuation that hangs in the air with them. 'I'm never violent. And I would never hurt you, Daisy, you know that. It's just men like that,' he says, jabbing a finger towards the floor, 'they shouldn't be allowed to get away with it.'

I drop on to the sofa, where the water from the burst pipe has seeped through and stained the bottom of the upholstery.

'What are you going to do?' he asks.

'That's for me to worry about.'

'Daisy,' he says, sitting next to me and reaching for my arm. I pull away, not wanting him near me. 'I didn't mean to cause you trouble. I just couldn't stand to hear him talk to you like that. And after him being in here... going through your things...'

He senses that I don't want to have this conversation now.

'Do you still want me to leave?'

I nod. 'You'll be late for work if you don't.'

He sighs. 'You know where I am, if you need me. You can't stay here...it'll make you ill. There's a spare room at mine... please just think about it. I'm sorry.'

'I think it's best you just go.'

I go to the bedroom and close the door, listening as he gathers his things in the living room. When I hear the front door slam, I stand near the window and watch his car pull away from the kerb. He's right: I can't stay here. But I have no idea what else I can do.

SEVENTEEN

On the crisp white sheets of the budget chain hotel bed, I pull up Aisha's number on my phone and wait for her to answer. When she does, I tell her what happened last night at the flat and this morning with the plumber and then with Craig, and by the time I get up to the point at which Andrew is punching him in the face, I realise I've been talking at her for nearly half an hour.

'I'm so sorry,' I say. 'I haven't stopped rambling. How are things with you?'

'Fine,' she says, brushing aside the question. 'More to the point... are you okay?'

'Not really. I mean, the punch shocked me. It was so out of character for Andrew. He's always so calm and gentle.'

'With you. But you're not a pervy intruder with an attitude problem, so I suppose his treatment of you is bound to be a bit different.'

'Well, when you put it like that...'

'I suppose some people might find it romantic.'

'Is that the measure of a man's affection now? How quickly he can break a pervert's nose?'

Aisha laughs, though it hadn't been intended as humorous.

'He was protecting your honour. It was a fight for decency. One man's quest for justice in the face of misogyny.'

'You know, if you slow that down and say it with an American accent, it'd make a brilliant movie-trailer voice-over.'

Aisha laughs again, and this time I don't mind.

'Honestly, though,' she says, 'I think he meant well. It might have been impulsive, but at least you know he'll defend you.'

I suppose Aisha is right, and I feel bad now for speaking to Andrew the way I did earlier at the flat. He did what he thought was right in the moment, and we've all at some point made a bad choice when faced with a split-second decision. He'd accepted being called a moron by Craig without any flicker of a reaction. It was him calling me a bitch that had made Andrew snap.

'Where are you now?'

'The Travelodge.'

'How much is that costing?'

'Too much.'

I hear Aisha sigh. 'I'm so sorry, Daisy. If I was still at my place, you could have come and stayed, but there's just not enough room here, and with Dada the way he is—'

'It's fine. Honestly, this isn't your problem... you've got enough to be dealing with.'

'How long will the repair work take?'

'From what the plumber said, I'm guessing at least a week. Maybe two.'

'Who's responsible for the costs?'

'I don't know. I mean, Andrew offered straight away to pay for it, but I think I'll go to Citizens' Advice, see what they say.'

I hear my phone ping with a message, and I move it away from my head to see who it's from. Andrew.

'You need to find somewhere else to live,' Aisha tells me. 'I know you don't want to go any further up the valleys, but it's got to be better than living with that piece of shit as your landlord.'

I know she's right. But with the cost of now having to stay somewhere else while the repairs are being carried out, I don't know how I'm going to afford to even put down a deposit on anywhere half decent or within a reasonable commute to work. I've never confided in Aisha about how much debt my father had left when he died. People have always assumed that my brother and I were left with whatever equity was in the family home, and as it's no one else's business, I've never bothered to correct the assumption.

There's a second ping on my phone.

'Look,' I say, 'I'm sorry I offloaded all this on to you. Shall we meet tomorrow morning before work?'

'Good idea. I'll meet you at nine in Costa Coffee.'

'See you there,' I tell her.

'But if you need anything between now and then, just call, okay?'

'Okay. Thanks.'

Once the call is ended, I check my messages. Both are from Andrew.

I know you're angry with me, and I understand why. I reacted impulsively this afternoon, and I shouldn't have done what I did. I can't stand the thought of anyone disrespecting you, but I also know you're right when you say you don't need me to fight your battles. I'm sorry I've messed things up x

And then the second.

I hope you can forgive me x

I put my phone on the duvet beside me and let out a long sigh. My thoughts are so conflicted. I can't stay here – even in a budget room and with a saver rate, tonight alone is costing me eighty-six pounds. That's over a quarter of my weekly take-home pay. And despite my shock today at Andrew's capacity for violence, I don't want things between us to end. We all have a breaking point, I suppose. And God knows, I'm not perfect. He has never shown me anything but kindness. As Aisha pointed out... I'm *not* Craig. There would never be any reason for Andrew to treat me in a similar way.

I pick up my phone and go back to his messages, reading them over another three times. Then I write a reply, editing and erasing several times before I send one that I'm happy with.

There's nothing to forgive. I know you were only looking out for me, and I'm sorry I reacted the way I did. I hate violence, but I understand why you hit him x

I wait a while for a reply to come, and when it doesn't, I worry that my response was sent too late. Perhaps he's decided that we're not right after all, and that today was a demonstration of our incompatibility. Despite having asked for my forgiveness, maybe he's had time for a change of heart. Should I be asking for his? I don't feel too sure of anything.

All I know is that I fall asleep with the phone in the bed beside me, still waiting for a response.

EIGHTEEN

Just before my shift ends, Andrew appears on the escalator coming up to the first floor. I didn't hear from him until 9.30 this morning, by which time I'd overthought things so much that I'd already told Aisha it looked likely things were over between us. I wasn't prepared for just how empty it had left me feeling, so when I see him, my heart swells with relief.

He spots me organising a display of women's coats.

'You didn't say you were coming.'

'I didn't know whether I'd be able to, but I managed to finish work early. I'm going to drive you to the flat – you can collect whatever you need. Come and stay at mine for a while, just until things at the flat are sorted. I'm so sorry about everything.'

He does look genuinely apologetic. And tired. Perhaps we had as little sleep as one another last night.

'Please don't apologise anymore.'

'Will you stay then? It'll take the financial pressure off you.'

'What about your mum?'

'She's fine with it. She thinks it makes sense. And I've had a bollocking for being so clumsy with that bloody drill.'

I check the time. Three minutes until I'm due to clock off.

'Maybe just a couple of nights then, is that okay? Just until I can find out what Craig's planning to do. I don't know why he didn't just let us sort it out with the plumber we'd called round – it would have saved him a lot of hassle.'

Andrew waves a hand dismissively. 'Don't worry about Craig.'

'There was something I didn't ask you, too. The evidence you said we had – the proof of him being in the flat. What was it?'

Andrew shrugs. 'No idea. But the threat did the trick, didn't it?'

Something about his casual dishonesty doesn't sit right in my stomach.

'Look,' he says, sensing my unease, 'as soon as I told him we had something we could take to the police, the panic on his face was instant. What does that tell you?'

'That he's guilty.'

'Exactly. He may as well have confessed to having been in your flat.' His eyes search mine imploringly. 'You said you saw a light flash. Maybe there still is a camera, somewhere. We're not the ones in the wrong here, Daisy.'

'I know. You're right. I'm sorry.'

'You've nothing to be sorry about. Look, I'll wait for you outside, okay. Don't worry about anything.'

I clock off in the staff room and collect my coat and overnight bag with the things I'd taken with me to the hotel. On the drive to Pontypridd, Andrew explains why he hadn't texted back last night, telling me he went to bed early in the hope that by starting work first thing this morning he'd be able to take the afternoon off and come to help me. We talk about the flat, about Craig and the state of the place even prior to the burst pipe, and Andrew makes me promise that while I'm staying with him, I'll let him help me look for somewhere nicer to live. He's so enthusiastic about the idea of helping me that I don't have the heart to tell him I've spent the last two years looking, and that there's nowhere available within my paltry budget.

When we get to the flat, Craig's not home. Or if he is, he doesn't want to answer the door to me. When we go upstairs, the smell of damp hits me instantly. It seems to seep from the walls and the furniture, hanging in the air like fumes. The framed print that Andrew bought for me is still resting against the far wall, thankfully devoid of any water damage. I pick it up to move it into the bedroom, away from the damp.

'Have you got a suitcase?' Andrew asks.

'No. I've got a rucksack.'

The admission creates an awkward silence for a moment.

After I'd got back from Spain, I'd got rid of everything that had been on that trip with me, from the suitcase I'd taken to the clothes I'd worn. I'd deleted every photograph that had been taken there, and I'd burned my passport. I would never need any of those things again.

'I've got some shopping bags in the boot of the car, if you need them?'

I nod. 'Thanks.'

I carry the print into the bedroom. I won't need to take too much for now, though I'll need more than I managed with overnight. Enough changes of clothing to see me through the next few days, toiletries, chargers; my laptop. I sit on the bed, looking around the sparsely furnished room. It all seems so pitifully pathetic. I am thirty-one years old. By this age, some people have navigated career paths that have seen them climb a steady ladder to success. Others have travelled the world, gaining a wealth of experience and excitement on their way. Some have got married and started families. I have nothing to show for my time on this earth, other than a history of tragedy and a head full of trauma.

'Hey. You okay?' Andrew appears at the bedroom doorway,

carrying a collection of bags for life. 'Blame my mother,' he says, putting them on the bed. 'You can never have too many, apparently.'

I can't imagine Rachel ever carrying around a shopping bag that has a cartoon of a smiling-faced cantaloupe with the caption 'Don't be a melon', but I say nothing.

I go to the chest of drawers, busying myself in the hope he won't notice the sheen of tears that have pinched at my eyes. 'I don't need too much,' I say, overly cheerily. 'Just enough clothes, really.'

'I can always bring you back if you forget something.'

Andrew waits for me as I pack up my few belongings. When we go downstairs, it's difficult to explain the feeling I get as the door to the flat falls shut behind me. This place is where I've attempted to rebuild my life. All Andrew sees is damp and mould, and an angry landlord with a short stature and an even shorter fuse. He doesn't have the emotional connection I feel to the place, so when he asks me in the car why I've gone so quiet, I can't tell him that it's because I have the unnerving sense that I might never see the place again.

NINETEEN

When we get to Andrew's house, Rachel is there. There's a radio on in the kitchen and we hear her singing as we step through the front door. A spicy aroma fills the air.

'She knows I'm coming?' I double-check in a whisper.

Andrew nods. 'I called her earlier to let her know what's happened, just so she knew you'd be here.'

I feel like a kid on a school exchange as I stand in the hallway with my overnight bag at my feet, something vaguely pathetic and desperate about this whole scenario. I wonder if I'd feel the same if Rachel wasn't here, and if I was just coming to stay with Andrew for a few nights. I doubt it.

'Hello there,' she greets us, hearing us in the hallway. 'Daisy, I'm so sorry about my idiot son. I tried to teach him basic DIY, but clearly we skipped the lesson on how to handle a drill.'

I smile, though I'm struggling to find the funny side of what's happened. I suppose this is just some people's way of dealing with things. I excuse Rachel's ill-timed banter with thoughts that this is exactly the kind of thing Aisha does as a form of self-preservation.

'It's no one's fault,' I say casually, as Andrew takes my coat from me.

Rachel is dressed for a night out, in a fitted top with a cut-out design around one shoulder and leather trousers that most women would look awful in, me included. She doesn't look like someone whose evening plans were dinner at home with her son.

'I've made a curry,' Rachel announces. 'I hope you like curry, Daisy? I'm sorry, I should have checked.'

'Curry's great. I'm not fussy.'

Rachel shoots Andrew a raised eyebrow look, and I'm left wondering what it insinuated. The thought rankles as I follow him down to the kitchen, where Rachel has set the table as though about to host a banquet. There are pillar candles burning at the centre of the table, wine glasses beside a decanter bottle; even napkins slid into little gold holders that are decorated with what looks from here like peacocks. I can't imagine the effort this woman must go into for Christmas Day.

The thought hits me like a slap. God, it's only a matter of weeks away.

'You really shouldn't have gone to all this effort.'

'It's nothing,' she says, dismissing the comment with a wave of her hand. 'I was cooking anyway. Do you fancy a glass of wine, you two?'

We both accept the suggestion, and Andrew offers to sort out the drinks while his mother finishes preparing the food. All I feel like doing is going to bed, but I'm locked into this dinner now, and I'm wondering whether I could make an excuse about not feeling well to get away from here once the food's been eaten. I imagine that might seem offensive to Rachel's culinary efforts.

'So, Daisy,' she says, once we've started eating. 'Tell us a bit about yourself. We know where you work and where you live, but what about *you*? Did you grow up locally?'

'Further up the valleys.'

'Whereabouts? I know the valleys pretty well... I had an auntie who lived in Treherbert, do you know it?'

I nod. 'I grew up in Tonypandy.'

'Not too far then. Are you an only child?'

'Mum...' Andrew intercepts with a tone of admonishment, because despite the innocence of the questions, it's quickly starting to feel like an interrogation.

'It's fine,' I say. 'No. I've got a brother.'

I spear a chunk of chicken with a fork as I feel the heat rising in my chest. I don't want to talk about my brother with people I barely yet know.

'How long have you been living here?' I ask, keen to move the focus away from my life.

'I've been here for about six months, but when did you buy the place, Andrew?'

'In 2018.' He gestures to the wine bottle, and when I nod, he tops up my glass.

'Thank you.' Six months? I didn't realise Rachel had been here for that long. I'd assumed when I'd first met her that it was only a recent thing.

Rachel pushes the food around her plate, having barely seemed to have eaten any of it. 'And what about work? Have you been there long?'

'Nearly five years.'

'You must enjoy it then?'

'It pays the bills.' I take a drink and turn the conversation back to her. 'What about you, Rachel? What do you do for work?'

'Oh, I'm between jobs at the moment. Is this a little too spicy for you? I hope I didn't put in too many chillies.'

I glance at Andrew, wondering whether he's noticed the way in which his mother has once again so deftly directed the conversation. If he has, he offers no reaction. He smiles at me, and I feel his foot find mine beneath the table, his toes moving up to my ankle and then my shin.

'Thank you for dinner,' I say, once Andrew and I have finished. Rachel claims to be full, having eaten less than half her meal.

'My pleasure,' she says, reaching over for my empty plate. 'I'm glad you enjoyed it.'

'Please let me do the dishes.'

Rachel laughs. 'That's what dishwashers are for.'

There's almost a sneer in the statement, as though she thinks me common for suggesting I wash-up by hand, though perhaps I'm just being paranoid.

'Shall I show you your room?' Andrew suggests.

'If you need any toiletries or anything, please help yourself in the bathroom,' Rachel tells me.

'Thank you.'

I follow Andrew out into the hallway.

'I'm so sorry,' he mouths.

I follow him upstairs, and he waits until we're on the landing to explain.

'I had no idea my mother was planning dinner like this. And I don't think she always realises how nosy she seems.'

'It's fine. Honestly, don't worry about it.'

He shows me to the spare bedroom, which is decorated with beautiful soft bedding. I want nothing more than to collapse beneath the duvet and drift into sleep. Andrew shows me where his room is and tells me I can use the en suite there. I'm grateful for the suggestion; if Rachel uses the main bathroom further down the corridor, I don't want to be invading her space. He goes back downstairs while I take a shower, and after getting dressed in a comfy pair of leggings and a T-shirt, I go back downstairs. It would be impolite for me to go to bed now.

I don't think either of them hears me come back into the

kitchen. They're both at the far side of the room, by the enormous American-style fridge, their heads close to mask their conversation.

'... went well, don't you think?' I hear Rachel say.

'Just ease off a bit though. You don't need to be so intense.'

'I borrowed a towel from the bathroom cupboard... I hope that was okay.' They both turn sharply when they hear me at the kitchen door.

'Of course,' Andrew says, coming over to me. 'Help yourself to whatever you need.'

We go into the living room, and I'm grateful when Rachel allows us some space. We talk for a while until I'm no longer able to suppress my yawns.

'Go to bed,' Andrew says, before kissing me. 'You know where I am if you need anything.'

I brush my teeth in his en suite bathroom and think how tempting it is to get into his bed and wait for him there. But with his mother just along the corridor it feels strange and inappropriate. Instead, I go to the spare room and lie in the dark, my mind lingering on the flat and all the possible things that might still go wrong.

My phone vibrates on the bedside table. Andrew.

You still awake?

Yes, I message back.

I'm so sorry again about my mother this evening, his reply comes quickly.

It's honestly fine. She was just trying to be nice by showing an interest.

Although in truth, it was a little overbearing. Perhaps a lot. It might just be that she was keen to impress me. Whatever it was, I'm sure Andrew will speak to her about it when I'm not around.

Is your room cold?

No, I reply.

Are you sure? quickly comes his response.

I smile as I realise what he's doing.

What if I said it was a little bit chilly?

I'd offer to come and warm you up.

I tap out a reply, grinning in the light of the phone screen beneath the duvet as I press send.

It's freezing in here.

No reply comes. I put the phone on the bedside table, and a moment later, the door is eased gently open, a beam of soft moonlight falling into the bedroom from the landing window. I see the shape of Andrew come into the room, then he pushes the door closed behind him, clicking the room back into darkness.

He says nothing as he slides beneath the duvet and pulls my body close to his. His mouth finds mine before his hands slide to my thighs, and I'm suddenly no longer as tired as I was.

'What about your mum?' I whisper.

'I'll try to keep the noise down,' he jokes.

'Shhh!' I laugh, but his mouth quickly stifles the sound. For the next hour his hands and his tongue make me forget who and where I am, and there's a part of me that hopes Rachel overhears us.

TWENTY

I'm leaving the bathroom when I hear Rachel call my name. She appears from the bedroom with a towel wrapped around her head, her hair freshly washed. Even from this far away along the landing, I can smell her expensive perfume. I'm pretty sure it's not the one Andrew bought for her on the day we first met.

'Andrew's working late tonight,' she says.

'Yes. He told me.'

'I was wondering, if you've not got any other plans... do you fancy going for a drink?'

The invitation catches me off guard. She was so intense at dinner last night, and I'm sure she must have picked up on my hostility towards her interrogation. Perhaps Andrew has already spoken to her about it, and she realises how full-on she seemed. Whatever conversation was started in the kitchen, my return to the room had cut it short.

'Look, about last night at dinner,' she says, disconcertingly appearing to have somehow read my thoughts. 'I'm sorry. I realise I might have come across as nosy... I didn't mean to be.'

I appreciate the apology. At first impression, Rachel doesn't seem the type of person who might part with them easily.

'It's fine,' I tell her, not really wanting to get into a conversation about it.

'Andrew has always told me I'm too nosy. Curious, I prefer to call it. Anyway... what do you think? Has Andrew taken you to the White Horse yet? It's got a lovely seating area by an open fire... if we get there early enough, we might get a table.'

And just like that, without me having had to offer a response to her invitation, I'm apparently going for a drink tonight with my boyfriend's mother. I try to think of an excuse to get out of it, but even if I find one, I'd then have to leave the house for the evening, and I don't really have anywhere to go. Finding somewhere would inevitably mean having to spend yet more money.

I finish my shift at 4 p.m. and get back to Andrew's house at nearly 5.30 p.m. His car isn't on the drive, so I presume his late night tonight must involve meetings somewhere. When I go inside, Rachel is in the kitchen. She's already dressed for our evening out, looking effortlessly glamorous in a pair of skintight leather-look trousers and an off-the-shoulder sweater. The woman manages to scream sexy in a way girls ten years younger than me struggle to pull off without looking desperate.

'How was your day?' she asks, passing me an empty wine glass. 'I thought we could have a cheeky one or two before we head out.'

'Too much Christmas,' I say, as she goes to the fridge and pulls a bottle of white from the door. 'I'm Christmassed out already.'

'Where do you usually spend Christmas?' Rachel comes back to the table and fills my glass before doing the same with her own.

I sip the drink before answering. 'With my brother.'

'Oh, lovely. Saves you doing the cooking, I suppose... wise move.'

I'd never said that I go to his, but I'm happy for Rachel to make her assumption providing it means we can move on to a different topic of conversation.

'Lovely handbag,' she says, gesturing to the one I've placed on the table beside me.

'A loan,' I tell her. 'From a friend at work.'

She looks at me pityingly, and I can almost see what she's thinking. *What a mess... can't even afford to buy herself a new handbag when her old one gets stolen.*

Rachel places a hand over mine. 'You know, please don't worry about all this business with the flat. I know it's worse than you'd both realised, but Andrew will get it all sorted for you. And you're welcome to stay here as long as you need to.'

I smile and say nothing. I don't need Andrew to sort things out for me, and I'm sure Rachel isn't the type of person who needs reminding that men don't hold the key to a woman's survival. Given her background, she of all women already knows as much.

And why is she telling me that I'm welcome to stay here for as long as I need to? This is Andrew's house... surely he's the one who should be making such offers, if he wants to.

I slip my hand from under hers, feeling awkward at the casualness of her physical contact. Some people are just tactile like that, but I barely know this woman. I ask about her day, keen to shift the focus from myself. Thankfully, it seems Rachel enjoys talking about herself, and while we get through our drinks, she regales me with an anecdote about a former colleague who's been trying to rekindle a friendship after sabotaging her chances at promotion.

'I'd better go and get ready,' I tell her, once my glass is empty.

'Okay, great. Wear comfy shoes – it's only a mile down the road, we can walk there.'

The walk turns out to be a pleasant one, despite the cold.

We bypass the main roads via a series of lanes that run along the backs of the terraced houses at the centre of the village, and within twenty minutes we've reached the pub. Rachel was right about the White Horse – it's like something from a Christmas romcom. The bar is decorated beautifully, with ornate garlands hanging low beneath the shelves of wine glasses, and an enormous real tree stands in the corner, lit with warm golden lights. Rachel weaves her way between tables to bag an available one near the fireside – a low table with an oversized armchair at either side.

'Bingo,' she says, as I slip my coat off and sit opposite her. 'This was exactly what I had in mind.'

'It's a really lovely place.'

'Isn't it? And they do cocktails too. There's an amazing one with elderflower – I've forgotten the name of it. Would you like to try one?'

'Let me get them in,' I say, standing.

'Absolutely not,' she says, stopping me with a hand on my arm.

'You've already been so generous.'

'Pfft,' she says, batting the suggestion away with a perfectly manicured hand. 'I haven't done anything. Come on... let me treat you. You can get the next ones in.'

I watch her head to the bar, in awe of her confidence and her presence. At the bar, she speaks casually and flirts with the younger barman, throwing her head back in laughter when he says something I can't make out from this distance. I find a disconcerting doubt creep over me. Is this where Andrew has learned his charm? When I'm not around to witness it, is this how he is with other women?

Stop it, Daisy. The man is not his mother.

When she returns to her table, Rachel passes me a long glass filled with a pale liquid the colour of diluted lime juice.

'I promise you,' she says, as she sits down, 'you will not be disappointed.'

She isn't wrong. The drink is delicious, and as the warmth of the alcohol flows through my bloodstream and the conversation picks up without awkwardness, I find myself relaxing and shaking off the concerns that just moments ago had bothered me.

'Things seem to be going well between you and Andrew.'

I nod. 'I think so. I mean, I hope so, anyway.'

'He's quite vulnerable beneath it all,' she says. 'You wouldn't know it... not many people do. He comes across as confident, but he's really quite unsure of himself at times. He never seems to know what he really wants.'

She looks me in the eye and smiles. I can't read her, but I know the comment's intention carries far more than its word count.

'Do you want children, Daisy?'

I almost choke on a mouthful of the cocktail. The question is so personal and so unexpected – so impertinent – that I take too long to react to it, and I'm annoyed with myself when I feel my cheeks begin to flush.

'I've never met someone I wanted to have children with.'

Rachel smiles. 'Clever answer. Sensible, too. Everything changes when you have a child. You lose a part of yourself that you'll never get back.'

Her left hand tightens around the bottom of her cocktail glass. For the first time, I notice it. The indentation around the third finger, left by a wedding or engagement ring. Andrew had mentioned Rachel's recent relationship breakdown.

'I would do anything for my son,' she says, leaning towards me, her eye contact unnervingly intense. 'Anything.' And then she sits back, like nothing happened. As though the abrasive tone with which the comment had been made was completely normal amid the rest of the evening.

'Another drink?' she asks cheerily, reaching for her empty glass. 'Same again?'

I probably shouldn't, and I'm not sure what the hell just happened there, but I don't want to seem rude, and I don't want to cause an atmosphere between us, not while we're temporarily living together. I'll just drink half of another, so it won't affect me in the morning.

'Thanks.'

'I've not seen Andrew this happy in a long time,' Rachel says, as she pushes her chair back to stand. 'Don't fuck it up.'

I stare at her back in disbelief as she walks away to the bar. For a moment, I think I must have heard her incorrectly. She surely can't have just spoken to me like that. And as I watch her at the bar, flirting outright once again with the barman who must be half her age, I think I must have got it wrong. She couldn't have just said that to me and now be acting like nothing happened... could she?

By the time Rachel returns with our drinks, I've resolved to ask her outright. 'What did you just say?'

'When?'

'Just now, before you went to get the drinks. You told me you haven't seen Andrew this happy in a long time, and then you said something else after it.'

'Oh,' she says, taking the slice of orange from the edge of her cocktail glass before sucking on it delicately. 'That. I said don't lock it up. You know... your feelings for him. I get the impression you might be on your guard a bit.' She reaches over to take my hand in hers. 'It's natural... we've all been burned in the past. But you don't need to hold back with Andrew. He's one of the good ones.'

Her eyes haven't moved from mine, and in all the time she's spoken, she's not once looked to the left or downwards. If she's lying, she's kept any evidence of it carefully concealed. There's something about this woman that's telling me she has no problem with lying to a person's face. And as she squeezes my fingers so tightly that the tips begin to turn pale, I'm certain of at least one thing: I know that isn't what she said.

TWENTY-ONE

When I go to the flat on Sunday it looks no different to when I last saw the place. If Craig's plumber has made a start on the repair work, he's taking his time about it. I doubt anything's been done; I know enough of Craig to realise he'll be sending me a bill for the work, and he'll probably be asking for at least part of the money up front.

I manage to catch him at home. He answers the door with his usual charismatic demeanour, but at least this time he's fully dressed.

'I need to know when the work's starting,' I tell him.

He looks me up and down slowly, his gaze dragging the length of my body. It makes my skin crawl.

'Busy time of year for plumbers.'

I bite my tongue. He was never going to make this easy for me. He's still pissed off with me for calling the police out, and despite the mess the burst pipe caused, I'd bet he was rubbing his hands at the opportunity to use it against me to make life difficult.

'Actually, I've got something for you.' He disappears into the flat for a moment and returns with an envelope.

'What's this?'

His piggy eyes narrow. 'You can read by yourself, can't you?'

I tear open the envelope and pull out the single sheet of paper folded inside. The first thing I see are the words 'Section 8 Eviction Notice'. I keep my focus on the letter, not wanting to give Craig the satisfaction of seeing my reaction. Key phrases stand out from the rest of the text: unauthorised alterations... breach of contract... repossession.

There are a hundred things I want to say to him in response to this, but my tongue is tied, and I can't believe that after everything – after the state in which he's left the place and allowed me to stay living – that he can treat me like this now. Yet I don't know why I'd expect any different from him.

'Best of luck trying to find someone else to move in.'

'You've got until the end of the week to get your things out.'

I go into the flat and slam the door behind me, standing with my back to the wall at the foot of the staircase as I try to catch my breath. I think about calling Andrew to ask his advice, but I don't want him to know about this, not yet. I told him I'd only be staying at his for a few days, and I don't want him to think anything's changed with regard to that. I won't outstay my welcome.

But nor do I have any idea where the hell I'm going to go.

I go upstairs and dig out an old backpack from the bottom of the wardrobe and fill it with as many clothes as I can. In the kitchen, I get two carrier bags from the cupboard beneath the sink and take the remaining toiletries from the bathroom. I've no idea how I'm going to get the bigger items from here. I could ask Andrew to bring his car over, but that's going to mean telling him what's happened. I need some time to think things through, but time is something I don't seem to have.

My phone bleeps in my pocket. As though he'd known I was thinking about him, it's a text from Andrew.

Everything okay? x

I check the time. He knew my shift was finishing at 6 p.m., and it's already gone 7.30. He's probably wondering where I am.

Went for a coffee with Aisha after work, I lie. *Be back in an hour or so* x

The print he bought me stands in the corner, throwing motion into the otherwise still living room. I realise now why it caught my eye as it did that evening in the restaurant, the freedom depicted in the image with its own romantic appeal. It would be nice to be able to just run away, all life's responsibilities melting into the tarmac as it fades from view. I sit staring at it for a couple of minutes, transfixed by the possibility of it. And then I realise I'm crying, and that I can't sit here wallowing in self-pity any longer.

I get a train from Pontypridd to Bridgend, lugging my backpack and carrier bags with me like a foreign exchange student who's managed to get lost. I walk the two miles from the station to Andrew's house, and when I let myself in through the front door, I head straight upstairs in the hope that neither he nor Rachel will see me with this stuff. I left this morning with just my coat and the handbag I borrowed from Aisha, so the extra bags are likely to raise questions. Luckily, neither of them is in the hallway or upstairs, so I manage to get to my bedroom and empty the bags before anyone realises that I'm here.

'Daisy.'

There's a tap at the bedroom door as I'm moving toiletries into the en suite.

'Long day?' Andrew asks, coming in and sitting on the bed.

'Yeah. I'm exhausted.'

'You must be hungry as well.'

'I ate with Aisha.' The lies are stacking up, and I hate the sound and feel of them. 'I feel like going straight to bed.'

His reaction shows no sign of any offence taken to this. 'Would you like me to bring you up a cup of tea?'

This man is just lovely. I can't recall either of my exes being this considerate. I'd find myself picking up after them or having to remind them of things that were their own responsibilities, sometimes feeling more like a parent than an equal.

'That would be lovely, thank you. Make two while you're there, though.'

He smiles and kisses me, and his lips on mine send a shock through my whole body. While he's gone, I get changed from my work clothes into a pair of pyjamas.

'I know you're tired,' Andrew says, when he returns with two mugs of tea and a packet of Hobnobs, as though he could get any more perfect, 'but there's a TV in my bedroom. Fancy watching a film, and if you fall asleep, I promise not to tell you what happens at the end.'

I take the warm mug from him. 'Sounds ideal. And I'm sorry... did you have better plans for this evening?'

'The fridge needs a clean out, but, you know, I'll let it wait... for you.'

I laugh, but inside I feel my stomach knot at the notion that I'm lying to him. I haven't told him about what happened with Craig this evening, or the eviction notice he so smugly handed me. I haven't told him that I now have nowhere to live. I'm staying here under false pretences, with him still thinking that I'll only be here for a few days.

When we go down the hallway to his bedroom, I wonder where Rachel is. I haven't heard her since I got in, and when I ask, Andrew tells me that she's gone to an aerobics class at the leisure centre. I get beneath his duvet, doubting I'll manage to keep my eyes open to stay awake through the first half an hour of a film. Andrew sits on the end of the bed and scrolls Netflix, asking me to choose something. They all look much the same, so

I land on something for the sake of recognising one of the actors, knowing that we're likely to talk through it anyway.

'How did last night go?' he asks, getting into bed beside me.

'Your mother hates me.'

Andrew looks shocked at the comment. I suppose after her inviting me out for a drink last night and coming home to tell him that we'd had a great time, to hear me suggest otherwise is likely to surprise.

'Why would you think that?'

'The way she is around me... I can just tell.'

Andrew shifts on to his side so that he's facing me. 'I know my mother better than anyone, and I guarantee that if she didn't like you, she wouldn't have you living in the same house as her.'

'This is your house though.'

'I know, but she'd make her feelings clearly known.'

He shifts the pillow beneath his head, while I wonder at how casually he's used the phrase 'living with'. This is only my third night here, and as far as he knows, could be one of my last. He's speaking as though it's a permanent thing, though it may just have been a turn of phrase.

'I won't be with you for long,' I remind him, feeling sick at the uncertainty that's hanging over my future.

'So while you're here,' he says, putting an arm around my waist, 'let me look after you, okay? And please stop thinking that my mother doesn't like you. She might have her guard up a bit, that wouldn't surprise me. That's just a reflection of her past – she's like it with everyone. People let her down her whole life, so maybe there is a part of her that's wary of anyone until she gets to know them. Her mother abandoned her to her grandmother, and then her grandmother died. There was a boyfriend she met when I was about eight or nine... they were together a few years, but then he cheated on her. That wasn't what she told me at the time – I found out afterwards. But look, what I'm trying to say is, she hasn't had it easy. Just give her time.'

Rachel's story is certainly one that evokes sympathy, yet despite it, I can't shake the feeling that there's just something off about her. And I can't get out of my head what I know she said to me in the pub last night.

TWENTY-TWO

On Monday morning, I get up late. The bed beside me is empty, and I wonder why Andrew didn't wake me up before he left for work. The stress of the flat has obviously left me exhausted enough to sleep far later than I would usually, and perhaps he'd thought that I needed the lie-in. There's plenty enough time before my shift this afternoon, so I get up and go downstairs. There's no one else here. Andrew told me he'd be working from the office today, and there's no sign of Rachel. I make myself a coffee and take it back upstairs with me, checking her room before going to Andrew's. She isn't here, and so I settle back into bed with my drink and call Aisha.

'How did Friday go?' I ask her, keen to hear how her date went. I feel bad for not having contacted her sooner to find out, but between my evening with Rachel and the trip to the flat, the weekend just ran away from me.

'Yeah,' she says casually. 'It was fine.'

Fine. An immediate indicator that all was not fine.

'Did you go somewhere nice?'

'Just some food. How's your weekend been? What's happening with the flat?'

For whatever reason, Aisha clearly doesn't want to talk about her date, and I know the worst thing I can do now is push her on the subject. She'll speak to me about it when she's ready to.

I tell her about Craig and my eviction notice, and I ask after her grandparents. I then remember there's something significant I haven't yet told her: what happened with Rachel on Saturday night. She listens silently as I relate the story, not speaking until I tell her about Rachel's 'don't fuck it up' comment.

'You're joking?' she says.

'You'd think so, wouldn't you? I mean, she tried to say that she'd said something else.'

Aisha tuts. 'Like what?'

'"Don't lock it up."'

'Yeah, okay. What does that even mean?'

'Exactly.'

'What do you think her problem is?' she asks.

'No idea. Maybe she's too used to having him all to herself.'

'Bit weird, isn't it?'

'Very. I mean, I might get it a bit more if she was older or vulnerable in some way, but Rachel is confident, capable, attractive... she should have her own life.'

'Where are you staying now?' Aisha asks. 'Look, I know what I said before about space, but you're welcome here. You'd have to bunk in with me, or I'll take the sofa – you can have my room. We'd make it work somehow.'

'That's really kind of you,' I tell her. But I know it's too much. Regardless of what she says, it wouldn't work. 'I'm at Andrew's until I sort something else out.'

There's a pause. 'That can't be easy with his mother there though, especially after what she said to you.'

'It's not going to be for long,' I tell her, hearing the lack of conviction in my words. I'm trying to take each day at a time, not to linger on the thought of how long I may be without a place of my own. But perhaps doing so is nothing more than burying my head in the sand.

I think I hear a noise from somewhere down the landing, and for a moment, I don't hear what Aisha is saying.

'Daisy,' she says, picking up on my momentary absence. 'Are you still there?'

'Yeah. Sorry. The line went funny,' I lie. 'What did you say?'

'I was just saying that it can't be comfortable for you now, staying in the same house after what she said to you on Saturday.'

'I don't see that much of her. It'll all work out somehow. Please don't worry about me, Aisha... you've got enough to be dealing with.' I change my mind about pressing the subject of her date, as much to steer the conversation from Rachel as to find out whether Aisha is okay.

'Are you sure you don't want to talk about Friday?'

'There's nothing to tell. My own fault... I broke the "never go back" rule.'

Something Aisha and I have always agreed on is that if a relationship didn't work out the first time, it's unlikely to do so given a second run. But Aisha had seemed to be looking forward to her date so much that I didn't want to mar it with the negativity of a reminder. She's been single for nearly three years now, and though she claims to love her independence, I also know she'd love to meet someone.

'Whatever happened,' I tell her, 'it's not your fault.'

'Yeah,' she says nonchalantly. 'On to the next one, I suppose.'

We end the conversation with a promise to try to catch up outside of work at some point this week, and when we've said goodbye, I put my phone on the bedside table. My half-drunk coffee has gone cold, so I take the mug with me out on to the landing. I try to think of something we could do together that might lift Aisha's spirits a bit – something cheap and cheerful that might help take her mind off everything else for a couple of hours.

I stop at the top of the staircase, my attention caught by a wet leaf on the floor near the front door. I don't remember seeing it there when I'd gone downstairs to make myself a coffee.

'Hello?' I say, wondering whether it's Rachel or Andrew who is back home, and just how much of my conversation with Aisha either one of them might have overheard.

But no answer comes back to me. The house is soaked in silence, with nothing more than the muted hum of the washing machine out in the utility room to break it.

I take the first step down the staircase, and it's then I feel a shove in the centre of my back, so swift and unexpected that I can do nothing to stop myself from hurtling towards the hallway floor.

TWENTY-THREE

'Daisy! Daisy!'

Andrew's voice is muffled and bubbling, as though I'm hearing him from under water. I feel arms beneath mine, and a pain cuts through my ankle as I'm lifted upright.

'What time is it?' I ask, unsure how long I've been at the bottom of the stairs. My first thought is that I can't afford to be late for work.

'Don't worry about that,' Andrew says, propping me against his legs as he sits at the bottom step. 'What happened?'

The pounding in my head is making me feel sick. I try to think back on how I ended up as I did, but everything seems blurry and fragmented.

'I'm fine,' I tell him.

With one arm around my back, he props me into a sitting position like a rag doll. The fingers of his free hand move across my skull, checking for possible injuries.

'We need to get you to the hospital. You might have concussion.'

'I'm fine.'

My earlier conversation with Aisha comes back to me in a flurry of details: her reluctance to talk about her date on Friday night, how she'd offered for me to stay with her; how I'd told her about Rachel and what had happened in the pub on Saturday evening.

Rachel.

'I was pushed.' I sit forward, almost losing my balance as I move away from the support of Andrew's legs.

'Whoa.' Andrew reaches for my shoulders and pulls me back towards him. 'Are you able to stand? Do you think you can make it to the car?'

'I don't need to go in the car.' But as soon as I try to stand, my efforts undermine the claim.

'Here,' Andrew says, putting one arm around my back and the other hand on my arm to support me. 'Don't worry about your shoes... I'll grab them once you're in the car.'

He helps me out of the front door and on to the driveway, where I get into the passenger seat, wincing with the pain that's spread through my right ankle. Andrew goes back into the house and reappears a minute later with my shoes, as well as a bottle of water, an apple and a cereal bar.

'Try to eat something.'

Going to the hospital seems an unnecessary fuss, but I don't have the energy to argue with him. I'm just aching, and although the pain in my ankle is severe enough to be distracting, it's probably a bad sprain rather than a break. I broke my wrist as a child once, trying to pull a gymnastics stunt on a metal railing. The pain then was so bad that I'd known straight away it was broken.

'I thought you were working from the office today.'

The clock on the dashboard tells me it's not yet 11 a.m. I try to think what time it had been when I'd called Aisha. I couldn't have been at the bottom of the stairs for more than an hour or so.

'I only had to go in for a meeting this morning,' Andrew tells me. 'Just as well I came back... you could have been there for hours.'

'I was pushed down the stairs,' I tell him, wondering whether he'd registered the words when they'd been spoken the first time around.

He glances at me as he slows for an approaching roundabout. 'What do you mean?'

'Exactly what I said,' I say, trying not to appear as frustrated as I feel. 'Just before I fell, I was shoved in the back.'

Andrew takes the second left and heads towards Llantrisant, where the nearest A&E department is. 'There was no one else in the house.'

'How do you know that?'

'I was at work.'

'Right... I know that. But your mother wasn't.'

I see his grip on the gear stick tighten, his knuckles turning white. 'What are you saying, Daisy?'

Is he being this obtuse on purpose? It's obvious what I'm saying, so I don't know why he's making me spell it out.

'I told you what happened in the pub with Rachel on Saturday night. I said last night that she hates me, and today she's proved it.'

He looks at me, incredulous. 'You seriously think she'd push you down a flight of stairs? Why?'

It's a reasonable question – one for which I have no answer. I don't know why Rachel has taken such a disliking to me, or why she would want to hurt me. All I know is, she did.

Andrew puts a hand on my knee. 'You've had a shock,' he says. 'It's understandable that things might seem jumbled—'

'Nothing's jumbled.' I push his hand from me. I know what he's suggesting – that the bump to the head has left me feeling confused, or that I'm concussed and remembering things differently to how they happened. But my head feels fine. The only pain I've got is the one in my ankle. That, and Rachel.

We don't speak for the rest of the journey to the hospital. After helping me hobble across the car park, Andrew gets me a wheelchair at A&E, and we wait an hour to see triage and then another for me to be taken for an X-ray and a head scan. I text my department manager, Claire, to explain why I won't be at work, telling her I fell down the stairs. I don't mention the push, and when she messages back, she tells me not to worry about anything and to look after myself. I reply with a promise that I'll make up the hours.

'Nothing broken,' the radiographer tells me. 'You were lucky. We'll get that ankle bandaged up and get you some painkillers. Are you allergic to anything?'

I shake my head. He leaves before returning with a prescription, then he gives Andrew the directions to the pharmacy, asking him to go and collect it for me. Things are still tense between Andrew and me; despite all the hours of waiting, he's barely spoken to me other than to ask if I'm okay and if I need anything. He doesn't want to admit the truth of what his mother is apparently capable of, and I can only hope that at some point he'll see her true colours for himself. But I know I can't stay around to wait until that happens.

'I'm sorry to have to ask this, Daisy,' the man says to me, once Andrew has left. 'It's routine when someone comes in after an accident such as yours, and I want to reassure you that this is a safe space. Is everything okay at home?'

I feel a tightening in my throat when I realise what the radiographer is suggesting.

'Yes. I mean... I don't live with Andrew. We're... I'm just staying there. Not for long. I just fell.'

His question has got me so perplexed that my ramblings are now making me look as though I'm lying. I'm inadvertently making Andrew look guilty.

He's not the problem, I want to say. It's his mother.

'I appreciate your concern,' I say, getting a grip on myself. 'But I'm honestly fine. Just clumsy, that's all.'

And as the words leave me, I hear them like he must: the classic line of a domestic abuse victim who can't yet speak out.

'Take this anyway,' he says, reaching to his desk before handing me a small card the size of a driver's licence, on which is printed a series of helpline numbers. 'Maybe put it somewhere safe,' he says kindly, from which I can translate, 'put it somewhere your partner won't find it'.

When Andrew returns with the prescription, I can't wait to get out of the place. In the car, he finally raises the subject of his mother again. Perhaps he hadn't wanted to talk about it in public, realising that what Rachel did this morning was criminal. Once again, he's protecting her.

'Look, what you said about my mother being there this morning... I'll talk to her, okay?'

'And you think she'll just admit to pushing me?'

'She wouldn't lie to me about something like that.'

I can't help the eye roll that escapes me, but I turn to face the window, sparing Andrew a portion of my scepticism.

'I don't believe she was there this morning,' he says.

'There seem to be lots of things you don't want to believe about your mother. It doesn't make them untrue, though.'

'She can be many things, but she's not violent.'

'Until today. You know I can't stay with you now, after this? I mean, what next? A razor blade in one of Rachel's jalfrezis? De-icer in my morning coffee?'

To anyone outside our conversation, I realise I must sound nuts. But I know what happened in that house this morning, and there is no one and nothing that can convince me otherwise.

Andrew looks as though he's about to respond in her

defence, but he apparently thinks better of it. 'Just let me look after you. Please.'

'I don't need looking after. I just need to be away from your mother. I'm sorry, Andrew... I don't think I can do this any more. It's me or her.'

TWENTY-FOUR

The following day, I go to work just to get away from Rachel. I managed to avoid her yesterday, going straight up to bed as soon as Andrew and I got back from the hospital, and allowing him to wait on me for the rest of the day as though I'd just given birth rather than been covertly assaulted by his mother. But within an hour of being there, I know I've made a mistake. The headache I'd barely felt yesterday is now raging at my temples, and I can only presume that after the fall, I'd been temporarily distracted from it by my swollen ankle.

At just before midday, Claire catches me coming out from the staff room, where I've just had to take another couple of paracetamols. The throbbing headache I woke up with has surged into a migraine, and all I want to do is lie in a dark room with a blanket over my head.

'You look terrible,' Claire tells me. 'No offence intended.'

'None taken. I feel it.'

'You shouldn't have come in today. Go home.'

'My shift isn't supposed to finish for another couple of hours.'

'It's fine, we'll manage. It's been quiet today anyway.'

I thank her and turn back to the staff room, not wanting to give her any time to change her mind. I get my things from my locker and head out of the store through the main customer entrance, as I always do now. The high street is quiet, with people presumably put off by the recent terrible weather. I don't even bother attempting to use the small umbrella that's in my handbag – the wind is so strong that it'll be blown inside out within seconds. Instead, I hold my hood in place while I make my way down to the train station, fantasising about the comfort of Andrew's spare bedroom and the nap I intend to take as soon as I get there.

The house is quiet when I get back. Andrew's car isn't on the drive. He told me he'd be working until six today. As for Rachel, I assume she's occupied with being 'between jobs', because, whatever it entails, it certainly seems to keep her busy. I wonder whether he's spoken to her yet. I'm sure I'll hear all about it as soon as he does.

In the kitchen, I get myself a glass of water and down it in three long gulps, desperate for some relief from the pain at my temples that's beginning to spread around to the back of my head. On the staircase, the injury to my ankle reminds me of its presence, the bandage the nurse had applied yesterday replaced with a new one after this morning's shower.

My plan to collapse in bed is put to an abrupt end when I find Rachel in my bedroom. It's the first time I've seen her since the fall – the *push* – yet she looks at me as though I'm the one who has no reason to be here.

'What are you doing?'

She's sitting on the side of the bed, facing away from the door. She couldn't have heard me come up the stairs, or if she did, she wasn't bothered about me finding her in here.

She turns to me, her long blonde hair – worn down today, in the kind of beach waves that look effortless but take an hour to style – sweeping across her shoulder as she reacts to my presence.

'Just taking a look at this,' she says, waving the paperback I'd left on the bedside table. 'I've been planning to get back into reading for a while now. Is it any good?'

She stands from the bed with the book still in her hand – the same hand that might have killed me just yesterday.

'To be honest,' she adds, turning the book between her fingers and making a show of absorbing the details of its front and back covers, 'I wouldn't have guessed this was your cup of tea. I'd have had you down as more of a crime thriller kind of girl.'

You don't know anything about me, I feel like saying, but instead I hold my tongue, refusing to bite to what feels like bait. Is she trying to goad me? It feels as though she's reminding me whose house this is, though I'm sure I've done nothing to suggest I believe otherwise. I wonder whether Andrew has spoken to her yet. I've given him an ultimatum, and I meant every word of it.

'"*Mr Right Now*",' she drawls, reading the book's title. She turns to the back. '"When recently jilted Annie MacBride arrives by accident in the small town of Heaven's Gate, love is the last thing on her mind. But a chance encounter with Nate Carter, the heir to the Carter-Hill real-estate empire, teaches Annie that life, and love, can lead to the most unexpected of places."'

She turns the book to look at its front cover.

'They're never poor, are they?'

'Who?'

'The leading men in these books. They never work for the council, do they? You never see a female protagonist fall head over heels for an ice-cream van driver.'

The temptation to make a Mr Whippy joke rests on the tip of my tongue.

'You can borrow it, if you like,' I say, trying to keep my tone from dropping into sarcasm. I know what she's trying to insinuate. She thinks I'm with Andrew for his money, or for this house, but I couldn't be less interested in whatever wealth he's gained for himself. I might be in a mess, but I've got myself out of them before and I can do it again, without the help of Andrew or anyone else.

'Thanks. Maybe pass it on once you've finished?'

I move into the room, and she registers my limp. 'What have you done to your leg?' she asks innocently.

She knows. She's aware of exactly what's wrong with my leg because she's the one who caused the injury. Yet to watch her now feign innocence, she's so convincing that anyone might believe her.

And if Andrew has spoken to her yet about the fact she needs to leave, Rachel isn't letting on.

'I fell down the stairs.' I exaggerate the word 'fell', letting her know that I'm on to her.

'Oh dear. You should really slow down, you know. I've watched how you rush about things... it won't come to any good.'

God, this woman is evil. I'd thought her interfering, overbearing, clingy... now, I'm sure she's the devil's less forgiving sister. Is she threatening me?

She moves towards the bedroom door, and I feel relief that she's leaving. Until, that is, I realise she's not.

'You don't mind me coming in here, do you, Daisy?'

She folds her arms across her chest, the attempt at fake casualness trying to belie the challenge in her words. Which answer would she prefer? I wonder. A compliant 'no' that will let her think she's winning here, or a defiant 'yes' that will help her prove to her son just how obstinate I am? Either way, I feel as though I can't win with this woman.

'What did you need to come in here for?'

She holds my gaze, still challenging me. I see a flicker of resentment in her eye when I fail to play along with whatever game this is she's playing.

'I was just looking for something. I haven't found it yet... but I will.'

She walks towards me, the book still in her hand. When she nears me, stepping so close that we're barely a foot apart, she thrusts the paperback at my chest.

'I look forward to reading it when you're done. You should finish it in Andrew's room... the light isn't so harsh in there.' She laughs. 'I mean, you don't sleep here anyway... you don't need two bedrooms.'

She saunters from the room, crosses the landing and heads down the stairs, while I bite my tongue so hard it feels I might draw blood. Exactly, I presume, what Rachel would wish for me.

TWENTY-FIVE

'Whoa,' Aisha says, her right eyebrow finally relaxing from the arch into which it's been raised throughout my retelling of what happened yesterday when I found Rachel in my bedroom. 'Okay... she was out of order.'

'Not just me then?'

'No way. While you're staying there, that's your private space. It sounds to me as though the book was just an excuse.'

That's what I'd thought too, but I hadn't wanted to come across as paranoid or defensive. And even had Rachel been going through my things, she wouldn't have found anything. Hardly any of my belongings are in Andrew's house; they're all still at the flat, because that's my home.

'Do you think she's feeling a bit threatened by you?'

'In what way?'

'I don't know,' Aisha says. 'Maybe she thinks that now you're there, Andrew might not want you to leave. Things are moving quickly between you.'

I feel a frisson of self-defence at the comment, as Rachel's words flood my brain. *I've seen how you rush about things.* 'What do you mean?'

'Nothing.' Aisha shoots me a look. She knows me well enough by now to have read my reaction. 'Things are going well though, aren't they? Maybe she's worried they're going so well she might have to start looking for somewhere else to live.'

I make sure no one else is around to overhear our conversation, before saying, 'She's already going to need to find somewhere else.'

Aisha's eyes widen. 'You're moving in with him? This is permanent?'

'She pushed me down the stairs.'

I watch as the words land, and for a moment I see what she can't conceal. Doubt. 'What?'

'After we spoke on the phone the other morning, she was there, in the house. I think she must have listened in on our conversation. I felt a hand on my back right before I fell.'

Aisha hesitates. 'Are you sure?'

'Yes,' I say, trying to withhold my frustration. 'And she knows I know... I can just tell.'

But Aisha is looking at me the same way Andrew had when we were in the car on the way to the hospital, like the blow to the head had sent me spiralling into paranoia.

She exhales noisily. 'Well... if you think she pushed you, you should report it to the police.'

'I've got no evidence.' Not yet, at least.

'But you're going to stay there?'

'Andrew's going to tell her she needs to leave.'

But Aisha looks as doubtful as I feel. Rachel's not going to leave without a fight, even if her son wants her to.

And I'm still not convinced that he wants her to go anywhere.

'Just be careful,' Aisha warns. 'You've only known these people a few months.'

'It's not him,' I say defensively. 'It's her.'

I don't know whether to feel affronted by Aisha's warning

tone. She knows from everything I've told her that Andrew has been nothing but good to me: kind and decent and generous. He's a good man. Perhaps that's the problem here. While there have been no kind and decent and generous men about, Aisha has had no competition for my time. And since her most recent date went badly, I'm beginning to wonder just how happy she really is for me.

'Daisy.'

I turn at my name, anticipating a rebuke for standing around talking while I'm supposed to be working. Claire approaches and asks Aisha if she could take over at the returns desk, but I get the impression it's just an excuse to get rid of her.

'The manager's requested to see you in his office.'

I frown, confused. I never have reason to go up to the office, and besides that, he's usually just called by his name: Dave. The formality makes it clear that whatever I'm being requested there for, it isn't good news.

'What about?' I ask, but she strides ahead as though she hasn't heard the question, and I follow her to the escalators, wondering what else this week has up its sleeve for me.

'Daisy.' Dave – the *manager* – greets me with a flamboyant spread of arms as I enter his office, looking uncomfortably as though he might pull me in for a hug. I hang back, just on the off chance. 'Take a seat.'

There's a cup of coffee on the desk that looks as though it might have been there for the past fortnight, and the layer of dust that coats the pile of paperwork beside it suggests he hasn't done any offline admin in perhaps as long. Claire takes a seat next to him.

'A complaint has been made against you.'

I look from one face to the other, waiting for one of them to deliver the punchline.

'Sorry?'

'By a customer.'

I feel my eyebrows furrow. 'I don't understand. What complaint?'

I try to think of anything that might have happened over these past few weeks – whether something I said or did could have been misconstrued by anyone. But there is nothing. I have no idea what they could be referring to.

'There's been an allegation of theft made against you.'

I laugh. 'Theft?'

'A customer claims to have seen you put an item of jewellery from one of the display cases into your pocket while you were on a shift.'

I sit in silence for a moment, dumbstruck.

'Theft?' I say again, apparently having lost the capability of speech beyond the parameters of a single syllable.

'Do you know which incident the customer may have been referring to?'

'Which incident?' I say, because it seems this meeting has turned me into a parrot. 'There is no "incident". I'm not a thief.'

'I understand this must be frustrating for you—' he continues.

'Because I haven't done anything.'

'But we have to investigate the matter.'

There's silence between the three of us for a moment, while both Dave and Claire wait for me to react further. 'Okay. So investigate. I look forward to hearing the findings.'

'The thing is, Daisy,' Claire says, 'company protocol is that while an issue such as this is being looked into, the member of staff in question can't be present at work.'

I look from one to the other again, at risk of starting to look as though I'm audience to a tennis match. Then I realise what she's saying to me. 'You're suspending me?'

'It's purely company procedure,' Dave tells me, relating the news like I'm supposed to feel reassured by the fact. 'On full pay, while an investigation into the allegation is carried out.'

I press my fingers to my lips, forcing back a reaction. I'm not sure whether I want to cry or scream, but either would offer some kind of release, and if I stay in this office a moment longer, I'm going to pass out either from the temperature or the nauseating expression of faux sympathy on the manager's face. Not so much from Claire, I notice, who's looking at me with eyes that say she already thinks I'm guilty.

'It begins with immediate effect though,' she adds.

My chair scrapes across the floor as I push it back to stand. I can't look either of them in the eye, and I realise as I leave the office that not doing so probably didn't do anything to help my case. If anything, it must have made me look guilty.

In the staff room, I fight back tears as I retrieve my things from my locker, making sure not to leave anything behind. No one speaks to me as I leave the building, and I'm for once grateful for the pre-Christmas crowds. For the first time since the night of the mugging, I leave the department store alone.

TWENTY-SIX

I try to hold it together on the way back to Andrew's house, but it takes such a monumental effort that by the time I get there, I've depleted my energy reserves. I get through the front door and, much to my horror, burst into tears. Luckily, there's no one here to see it. Or at least, I'd thought there wasn't. When I hear the flush in the downstairs toilet, I realise I'm not alone in the house. I hastily wipe my eyes to disguise my tears, but I'm not quick enough, and a moment later, Andrew appears in the hallway.

At least it isn't Rachel.

'Is everything okay? What's happened?'

He comes over to me and pulls me into a hug. He smells of the aftershave he always wears, and coffee.

'I think I've just lost my job.'

'What? How?'

He guides me to the dining table and pulls out a seat. Sitting next to me, he takes my hand in his and asks me what's happened. I tell him everything, from being called into the manager's office, to being told I'd need to take time off while the allegation is being investigated.

'This allegation,' he says. 'What is it?'

'Theft.'

'What? That's ridiculous.'

'To us. But apparently not to my bosses. Five years I've been working there. Surely that's long enough for them to know I'm not a thief.'

Andrew squeezes my fingers gently. 'I'm so sorry, Daisy. You don't deserve this. I'm sure it'll all get sorted out quickly. Once they realise there's no evidence to back up this allegation, they'll be apologising to you.'

I roll my eyes. 'I doubt that. I don't even want an apology... I just want to be able to go to work.'

Andrew gets up from the table and returns with a glass of water for me. 'Have you spoken to your mother yet?' I ask as he sits back down.

'Look, Daisy—'

'I knew it. I knew you wouldn't do it, or there'd be some excuse, and I can't st—'

'She wasn't here,' he cuts me short.

There's a moment of silence between us. I notice that where moments ago he was holding my hand, he's now keeping a distance between us.

'I heard a noise on the landing before I left the bedroom,' I tell him. 'She was waiting there for me.'

'But you didn't see her.' It's said as a statement rather than a question, and Andrew's tone is flat and matter-of-fact, leaving no room for negotiation. He reaches into his pocket and pulls out a small scrap of paper. 'She was shopping,' he says, handing me what I now realise is a receipt. Kurt Geiger, nonetheless.

'She was in the retail outlook off the M4 until after lunch. Look at the time,' he instructs me, pointing to the top corner of the receipt. 'So, she couldn't have been here, could she?'

I register the last three digits of the card used to make the purchase. 'This could be anyone's card.'

He reaches behind him and slides his phone from the worktop, apparently prepared for this counterargument. 'Look.' He pulls up two photos and swipes between them: the front and back of Rachel's bank card. The last three digits are a match. 'I don't want to keep these on here, so I'll delete them now, if that's okay with you.'

His tone is so cutting that I feel as though I'm somehow the one in the wrong here. Yet that's exactly what he believes, and now I'm also starting to.

'She wasn't here, Daisy.' He takes my hand in his again. 'Look, you're going through an awful lot at the moment. The upheaval of the flat... what's been going on with the landlord... now this business with your job. It's understandable that you're tired. We all make mistakes when we're tired.'

I put my fingertips to my temples, where yet another headache is raging.

'Look at you,' he says, running a hand across my knee. 'You're exhausted.'

He's right – I am. But I know what I heard. I know what I felt... don't I? And Rachel has been so odd with me, first the snide comment in the pub and then finding her in my room like I did. Whatever her problem is, she doesn't want Andrew and me to be happy.

'I can't stay here while she's here,' I tell him.

'And I can't ask her to leave. She hasn't done anything wrong.'

He pulls me into him, and I rest my pounding skull against his chest, too tired to object. My life is crumbling around me – first the flat, now my job – and it feels as though the only solid thing is Andrew. But between Rachel's vitriol and Aisha's resentment, it feels as though everyone wants to curse us before we've barely begun.

I need to prove Rachel's guilt, but I'm not sure I can.

Perhaps I can't prove anything, not while I'm unsure I can even trust my own memory of events.

TWENTY-SEVEN

'Come on,' Andrew says, pulling me from my reverie. 'Are you hungry? Let me take you for dinner somewhere, to cheer you up.'

'I don't think I'm up to it. I'll only be miserable... it'll be a waste of money.'

'What about a takeaway then?'

'Only if you let me pay for it.'

He ignores the comment and gets up from his chair. 'Why don't you go and get changed out of your work clothes... get a bit comfier. I'll make you a cup of tea.'

'You don't have to always be so nice to me.'

'I know,' he says, leaning down and kissing me. 'But I enjoy it. Let me look after you, Daisy. Go on... I'll put the kettle on.'

'Could I have a quick shower?' I ask him, planning to use the en-suite to avoid Rachel if she happens to come home earlier than expected.

'You can have a slow one if you like. Take your time.'

I leave the kitchen and go upstairs, heading first to my own room. I get a towel and a change of clothes, opting for a pair of leggings and an oversized jumper. A takeaway and a curl up on the sofa sounds a good attempt at taking my mind off my suspension from work, if only for a brief time, and I'm pretty sure that Rachel is out at her Pilates class tonight. It means Andrew and I will get the living room to ourselves, so we'll be able to watch a film.

I remove my work clothes and wrap a towel around me before pulling some clean clothes from my backpack, which I take with me down to Andrew's bedroom. The door is ajar, and even before I've entered the room, I smell something strong in the air, like wax melts. I don't know what to think when I open the door. Fairy lights have been strung from the picture rail, stretching the length of wall that runs behind the double bed. The bedding is different to the one that was there before, the nondescript grey duvet set replaced with a teal silk cover embroidered with an intricate floral design. And even worse... on top of it, pink rose petals have been strewn across the bed. On the bedside table, a bottle of Merlot sits beside two wine glasses. Next to them, there's an expensive-looking box of chocolates. The room looks like a film set from a cheesy 1990s romcom, and if I hadn't just been suspended from work, the weirdness of it all might be enough to make me laugh. Instead, I feel suffocated by it.

'Andrew!'

I call him twice before I hear his footsteps in the hallway downstairs.

'Everything okay?' he calls up.

'What's all this?' I call back.

He appears at the bottom of the staircase. 'Is the temperature playing up again?' he asks, seeing me standing with a towel wrapped around me. 'It sometimes takes a while to warm up.'

'I haven't made it to the shower yet. I just wanted to know what the bed was about.'

He pulls a face. 'What do you mean, what the bed was about?'

I pull the towel tighter around my chest, feeling cold and strangely exposed, wishing I'd gone and got dressed before I questioned him about the bedroom. 'Could you come up a minute?'

Andrew comes up the stairs and follows me down the landing to his bedroom.

'What the hell?' he says, when he enters the room and sees the bed.

I look at him questioningly, wondering whether this is still some kind of wind-up, but the expression on his face says he had no idea all this was here.

'I didn't do this,' he says quickly. 'I mean... where did that bedding come from? It's awful.'

'Andrew,' I begin, not in the mood for his attempt at playful banter.

'I got home not long before you did,' he tells me. 'I was working on my laptop in the living room. I didn't... I mean, this is not...'

He looks back at the bed, cringing at the scene that greets us there.

'So what you're telling me is that your mother did this?'

The words hang in the air between us for a moment, awkward as all hell. It sounds even weirder than it looks, now that it's been said out loud.

'Daisy, I am so sorry. This is embarrassing.'

I can't imagine that it's more embarrassing for him than it is for me, still standing here in a towel, waiting for a shower I'm now not going to take.

'This is probably her way of trying to make up for things.'

'What things?' I say, hearing the passive aggression in my words. 'According to you, she's not done anything wrong.'

'But she knows you've been feeling unsettled. Look, this isn't the most normal of ways to go about it, I admit, but I'm sure she's just trying to make you feel more at home here.'

I pull a face. 'By making things weird as hell?'

'I did just say it wasn't the most normal of things to do.'

I bite my tongue, because I know there'll be no coming back from what I really want to say. Instead, all I say is, 'I need to get dressed.'

I take my clothes with me into the en suite, and when I go back into the bedroom, Andrew has cleared the bed of the rose petals and removed the wine and glasses from the bedside table. The fairy lights have been turned off. He's sitting on the end of the bed, waiting for me.

'I don't know what the hell she was thinking.'

I say nothing, because there's nothing that I can think to say that won't make the moment any more awkward or uncomfortable for us both. He gets up and comes to me. 'I'll talk to her about this tonight. It's not okay.'

'It's really weird.'

His mouth twitches in reaction. 'I'm sure to her mind, she was just trying to be nice.'

I smile at his naivety. 'And what about yesterday, when I came home from work to find her in my bedroom?'

'She was in your room?'

'She claimed she was looking for something.'

'Like what?'

'Funnily enough, she didn't say. Convenient, that.'

'Okay,' Andrew says, taking me by the hand and sitting on the edge of the bed. I sit beside him. 'Maybe she was looking for something. I hadn't cleared the room out completely before you came to stay... there wasn't time. If you look in some of the drawers, there's still some stuff in them. That's my fault... I should have got it all cleared.'

I take my hand from his and sigh.

'What?'

'You always do this,' I tell him. 'You always defend her, no matter what she's done.'

'That's not true. I spoke to her about the way she was at dinner the other night, and I'll speak to her about this.'

'And I'm sure speaking to her will have a huge effect,' I say, unable to withhold the sarcasm. I head for the bedroom door. 'I need to go.'

'Go where?'

'Home.'

He follows me down to my room, where I start throwing the few possessions I'd brought here with me into my backpack. Andrew still doesn't know I've been given an eviction notice, and I still have a few days left to stay at the flat if I need to. I'll be warm enough in bed.

'Daisy, you can't stay at the flat – it'll be freezing.'

'It's pretty frosty here too,' I snipe.

'Please,' he says, holding me by the arms. 'I don't want you to go.'

I really need for his hand not to be touching my bare arms, because every time his skin is against mine, I seem to lose all my other senses. I don't want to go either, but I can't stay here while Rachel is still here.

'Please let me go.'

His fingers fall from my arm. I push my backpack on to my shoulder, feeling my heart thump beneath my T-shirt. I left my sweater somewhere earlier, but I can't remember where I put it. I'll need to find it before I leave, and Aisha's handbag too.

'If I tell you that I'm in love with you, will you stay then?'

My fingers slip from the handle of the bag.

'Not if you're saying it just to get me to stay.'

Andrew comes over to me and holds my face in his hands.

He smells of the aftershave he was wearing that first day on the train. Those bronze eyes that had drawn me in with that very first look at the department store hold me rapt once again, snared within their gaze.

'I'm saying it because I mean it. I love you, Daisy. I know we've only known each other a couple of months, but it's all I need. And I know this is only temporary, you staying here, but please, let me enjoy it while it lasts. I'll speak to my mother. I promise you we'll establish some boundaries.'

'I can't imagine that will go down well.'

'I don't care. I know she didn't push you down those stairs – she couldn't have, and she wouldn't have. But I agree with you about everything else – her behaviour has been weird. But it's not your fault. So please don't go.' He leans down and kisses me, his lips soft against mine. 'I've loved having you here. I know it was only meant to be for a short time, but I suppose I've let myself get carried away with things... with the idea of you being here. These last few days have been... I don't know... normal, I guess. And I mean that in the best way possible. I just can't imagine going back to not having you here.'

I feel a lump of guilt in my throat that I haven't yet told him about the eviction notice. I don't want him to regard me as vulnerable or needy, and I certainly don't want him to think that I'm becoming dependent on him.

'This isn't my home,' I remind him.

'I know. And I'm sorry. But, please... just let me be selfish while it lasts.'

He tilts my chin upwards so that I'm looking right at him, and I feel myself melt again beneath his gaze. I forget the backpack... I forget about leaving. When he presses me against the wall and his hands begin to search my body, I forget the eviction notice and the suspension from work. For a moment, I forget Rachel.

This man is like a drug, and I am the most willing of addicts.

I imagine hearing the front door and Rachel coming up the stairs, finding us like this. Unlike that second time I'd come to the house, I'd welcome the intrusion. I'd willingly have her catch us half-dressed and devouring each other, because she needs to realise that Andrew is no longer her little boy. And mummy dearest needs to see that I'm not going anywhere.

TWENTY-EIGHT

Liam doesn't want to communicate with me again today. I can usually tell within moments of arriving what the mood of our time together will be; there's a charge in the air, something that only he and I can sense. Today, he is drifted far beyond the point of detachment. Now, he is positively hostile. His staring eyes look past me, and when I take his hand in mine, there's a distance that I can just somehow feel.

With his head lolled to his shoulder, it shocks me today just how much older he looks. He turned twenty-eight in the summer, but the sag at his cheeks and the furrows that run deep across his forehead make him look like a middle-aged man. I feel a pang in my chest at the boy that has been lost. Because despite still being here, he's not, no matter what they say. There is a version of him, altered. The other, original Liam is gone forever, still submerged beneath that water.

He used to be such a good-looking boy. At school, the girls all loved him. He was obsessed with sport – football and hockey, in particular – and he was as popular with the teachers as he was with his classmates. He was never without friends, and he managed to navigate an entire school life without falling prey to bullying in even its supposedly mildest of forms. I was never a part of that time. Back then, he never wanted to be seen with me. But I watched him from afar, in admiration and with envy, wishing that I could be as capable as he already seemed to be.

'I met someone,' I tell him. If there's a reaction inside him somewhere, it remains hidden like every other. 'It's been a little while now… we're just getting to know each other. I think he might be one of the good ones.' I laugh, and the sound echoes around his sparsely decorated bedroom. 'God knows, there's not many of them about.'

Already, I've run out of things to say.

'Will you talk to me today?' I ask him. 'Please.'

A wait for a second blink, but it doesn't come. Elated by the unexpectedness of his response, I go to the drawer for his letter boards.

We repeat our familiar routine, and the boards shake in my hands with anticipation as I wait for each blink. I write each letter out in turn, awaiting what he wants to say to me.

Please stop.

'Please stop what?' I ask him, desperate to know what he's referring to. Does he want me to stop trying to get him to communicate?

And then something happens that has never happened before, something so unexpected that the letter board falls to the floor with a clatter. A growl escapes Liam's body. The sound is so sudden and so brief that for a moment I wonder whether I imagined it. But I didn't. I know I didn't. He is so angry with me… so full of contempt… it has enabled him to produce sound for the first time in five years.

I should be elated. I should be rushing down the corridor to find one of the nurses. I should be getting my mobile from my coat pocket and phoning someone, anyone, to share the news.

Instead, I sit rooted to the chair, too shocked to move. Because whatever else has been communicated, one thing has been made clear: Liam hates me.

'Liam,' I say gently, 'I don't know what you want me to stop doing. Let's go again.'

But when I pick up the board and move my fingers across the letters, I gain nothing more from him. I put the things back in the drawer and go down to the day room, needing a few minutes on my own.

There is no one here. Although it's designed for families to have more space to be able to spend time together, the sad fact is that this room is barely used. Patients often stay in their own rooms, and when families do visit, they never seem to stay for long.

I shut the door and sit in the chair closest to the window, overlooking the same view seen from Liam's bedroom. The noise he made echoes in my head, alien and inhuman. It couldn't have been him… and yet it was. The tears roll hot and heavy down my cheeks. This is what I didn't want, for him to see me upset like this. He doesn't deserve it, and it isn't fair. I owe it to him to try to make things right somehow, not to bring my misery here with me during our time together.

I thought that given time, I could make things better. I thought I could undo the wrongs I'm guilty of, that I could repair our relationship by atoning for the ways in which I let him down. But the more time I spend here, the more I come to fear that it's too late. And no matter what I try to do now, I know Liam still blames me for everything. He might not be able to say so, but I can feel it in the energy that still radiates from him, like a friction that rises on the air whenever I get too close to him.

Please stop.

He hates me. He blames me for what happened to him, and

he has every right to, because I know deep down, though I've been too scared to admit it even to myself, that his being here is all my fault. If it wasn't for me, he wouldn't have been there that day. I led him to a near-death, and then I abandoned him.

TWENTY-NINE

There's an atmosphere at dinner this evening, and it's one I can't wait to get away from. I don't know whether a meal together tonight was Andrew's idea or Rachel's, when it makes no sense for it to have come from either. Rachel clearly despises me, and after everything Andrew and I have discussed in relation to her, he should realise that being coerced into sitting at a table and making conversation with his mother is the last thing I want to face, especially after the disastrous nature of the rest of this week.

I told him last night about the eviction notice. He's promised not to mention anything to Rachel and has also promised not to tell her about the allegation made against me at work. The last thing I need is for her to think I'm a thief, particularly as she already appears to have me down as some kind of gold-digger who's planning to trap her son and trick him out of his worldly possessions.

Yet there's only so long I can keep away from the house during my supposed 'work' hours until she realises something is off. If she finds out I've been suspended, she might see my stay here as something I'm planning to make more permanent, and I don't want to give her more reason to resent me. All this couldn't have happened at a worse time, with Christmas just around the corner.

Tonight, Andrew cooks, and he allows me to help when I make the offer. I'm grateful for it: at the other side of the kitchen, I feel guarded from Rachel's judging eyes. When she asks about both our days, I'm forced to casually dismiss it as 'fine', as though I've been to work as normal. Yet I sense that somehow, she knows I'm lying.

She goes to the fridge and takes out a bottle of wine before setting three glasses on the worktop beside where I'm peeling carrots.

'I owe you an apology,' Rachel says, as she fills a glass and hands it to me. I feel the breath leave me as though it's been sucked into a vacuum. Is she finally going to admit to shoving me down the staircase?

'The other day,' she says, 'when I was in the spare bedroom, I was looking for an adaptor lead. I haven't needed it in months, but I've not been able to find it anywhere else.'

I take the glass from her and take a sip of wine. I could quite easily gulp the contents down in one, if it would mean an escape from this awkwardness. I'd known Andrew had spoken to her about it, but I hadn't expected her to raise the subject again, and certainly not with the three of us together. And I know she's lying about an adaptor lead.

I tell myself that at least she's acknowledging fault, yet her use of the phrase 'spare room' echoes at the front of my mind, and her apology immediately rings in my ear with a different tone. She may as well have told me to remain mindful of the fact that I am only a guest here, and a temporary one at that. And I notice she doesn't make an apology for, or mention of, the weirdness of the whole bed of roses and fairy lights set-up she'd left for us.

'I understand it must be different for you, having lived alone for so long. I'm sorry... I forget. Andrew and I are always in and out of each other's rooms if we need to borrow something... it's never been a problem. But when you've been on your own for so long, I can imagine your personal space becomes a little more sacred. Anyway... as I say, I'm sorry.'

'It's forgotten,' I say, telling yet another lie. I'm not likely to forget anything this woman says or does. In fact, I've started stacking her 'offences' in a mental filing system, easily accessible the next time Andrew tries to defend her boundary-crossing behaviour.

'Ladies,' Andrew says, approaching the dining table with two plates, 'my secret recipe chicken breasts with apricot chutney. *Bon appetit.*'

'What's the secret?' I ask, sitting at the table.

'It wouldn't be a secret if I told you, now, would it?'

He returns with his own plate, and the three of us eat in a semi-silence, the atmosphere punctuated with the occasional generic comment about our respective days. Until Rachel throws a festive-shaped bombshell into the mix.

'We need to discuss Christmas,' she says. 'It's right around the corner.'

'What do we need to discuss?' Andrew asks. 'It's usually a low-key affair for us.'

'Will you be having dinner again with your brother this year, Daisy?'

'I imagine so,' I say, feeling my pulse start to quicken in my chest. The thing with telling lies is that you need to remember the ones you've already told. 'I haven't given it much thought yet... there's been so much going on.'

'Of course. I imagine he'll be expecting you, though, if you're there every year. Do you see your brother very often, Daisy? You never really seem to talk about him.'

Shut up, I think. *Shut up, shut up, shut up.*

'You're obviously welcome to spend Christmas Day here too, if your plans change,' Andrew says to me.

A dark cloud passes over Rachel's face. I wait for her to say something in objection, but she can't. This isn't her house; it's not her decision to make.

I wonder whether Andrew spends every Christmas with his mother. Is this what normal families do? I imagine it must be, but I've not experienced it in so long that I don't know what a 'normal' Christmas looks like.

'I'm sure Daisy wouldn't want to let her brother down though, Andrew. Not if he's expecting her.'

Shut up, shut up, shut up.

In my head, the top of my skull has just burst open like a party popper, spraying strands of red bloodied ribbon across the cutlery and the ridiculous napkin holders. A wet tendril of brain matter has splattered on to Rachel's perfectly made-up face, her lipsticked mouth frozen in a tableau of undiluted horror. It is a macabre and glorious image.

In real life, I must appear to Andrew and his mother frozen with a grimace, trying to maintain a façade of calm amid yet another onslaught of Rachel's interrogation.

'We're both busy adults leading our own lives,' I say, spearing a stalk of tender stem broccoli with my fork as I swallow my sickness at the lie. 'It wouldn't be normal to live in each other's pockets, now, would it?'

I offer Rachel a sickly smile, relishing the reaction I can see within her cool grey eyes. I have rankled her, and I feel fucking overjoyed. Because this isn't 'normal', whatever I might have thought moments ago. Wanting to know the details of everything... wanting to buddy up to your adult son's girlfriend... snooping around among her things in the hope of finding... what? An adaptor lead?

'Actually, Daisy... now we're on the subject, I was wondering if you'd help me with an important job tonight?'

I catch Rachel's sceptical look as she eyes first her son and then me.

'Depends on what it is...'

'I thought you and I could put up the Christmas tree together.'

You and I. Andrew's deliberate exclusion of his mother turns Rachel's complexion practically puce. I reach for my glass and take a sip of wine to try to hide any reaction that might be showing on my own face. She is seething. She's doing her best to hide the fact, but her reaction is so intense she's unable to conceal it.

'You've got a tree?' she asks.

Andrew laughs awkwardly. 'What do you mean, "you've got a tree"? It's nearly Christmas, isn't it?'

Rachel grimaces. 'I mean... you've never had a tree before. I've never seen a tree here.'

'I never had anyone to put a tree up with before,' he says, shooting me a look. 'It feels different this year.'

Beneath the table, his foot finds mine. I feel like a teenager, and I relish in the momentary pleasure of having Andrew choose me over his mother. Putting up a Christmas tree together is a normal couples thing to do. But apparently, she doesn't see it in the same way.

Rachel pushes her chair back, despite her meal being barely half eaten. She snatches up her wine glass and refills it. 'Thank you for dinner,' she says frostily. 'I think I'll leave you two to it now. I wouldn't want to be in the way.'

I wait for Andrew to say something to pacify her, but for once, he just lets her go. We sit in silence until we hear her on the landing, and when she's gone to her bedroom like a sulking teenager, he gets up and closes the kitchen door.

'I'm so sorry.'

'Yeah... so you keep saying.' I sigh heavily, as though I've been holding my breath for the last five minutes. 'This isn't normal, Andrew. I know you're trying to help her out, but she's too involved with everything... I feel like I'm suffocating around her.'

'It's no different than what Aisha does for her family.'

I pull a face. I've spoken to Andrew about Aisha and her relationship with her grandparents, and I've no idea how he thinks this could be in any way similar to her situation.

'Aisha lives with her grandparents as a carer. Her grandfather is sick... he's vulnerable. There's nothing vulnerable about your mother.' But she is sick, I stop myself from adding.

'You don't have to be unwell to need help.'

'True. But you don't bite the hand that feeds you either, so if you're trying to help her then why does she keep making things so difficult for you?'

Andrew doesn't answer, maybe because there isn't anything to respond with. He's not the one she makes things difficult for. That, it seems, is saved purely for me. Why does she keep questioning me about my family? The interest in my brother has gone beyond the casual: this is the third time she's brought him up now, despite me already having told her everything she should need to know. Sometimes, she looks at me as though she's seeing more than Andrew can see, as though she somehow knows things I've never told either of them. And of this I'm certain: Rachel knows far more about me than she's letting on.

THIRTY

He is just inches from me, and yet I cannot get to him. My hands claw at the broken parts of the boat that surround us, struggling with the beam that lies across the lower half of his body, my fingertips bleeding as I claw at the rough wood and steel. The dance music that was still blasting from the speakers just minutes ago has finally died. In its place is a tide of panicked screaming and the rush of water as it fills the lower deck of the boat.

'It's going to be okay,' I hear myself say, and somewhere above the dream, as though looking down at myself in an out-of-body experience, I am screaming silently, no one able to hear me above the noise.

Stop lying to him. You are lying to him.

The water is up to his chest now. It was slow at first, seeping gradually through his shorts, but now he is sitting in a pool, and it continues to rise as I lie to him. Behind me, there's a gap in the fallen structure that was once the floor of the top deck. I'm pretty sure I could make it through the space, just about. But it would mean leaving him behind. I couldn't live with myself... could I?

The water is rising, and the screams are floating away... the others are being rescued, safer in the ocean than they are inside this shell of a so-called party cruise. He is trapped, but I am not, and an escape lies just behind me, but I don't know what to do and we are both going to drown here...

'Daisy!' There are hands are on my shoulders, shaking me. 'Daisy!'

I am snapped from sleep by Andrew, his face inches from mine.

'You're okay,' he says, pushing my sweat-slicked hair from my face. 'You're okay. Everything's okay. It was just a nightmare.'

He pulls me closer, and I curl into his side, my heart thundering in my chest as the water around me fades to a memory. Each time it comes, I wake with the same thought, that I could have done something differently. There must have been another way. The thought that perhaps there was some way I might have changed what happened haunts me, and I know it always will. The guilt is a weight I carry with me.

'What was it?' Andrew asks. 'What did you dream about?'

'I don't remember.'

I've never spoken to anyone about that day, other than the therapists I saw for a while, years ago. They couldn't help me. After a while, I realised we were just going around in circles, revisiting that day as though clinging to a hope that by going back there in my head I could reverse the outcome – as though regret alone would be enough to undo it. It didn't matter how many times I was told that what happened that day wasn't my fault... that no one could have prevented the accident... I might have heard it, but I could never believe it.

Aisha knows about the accident, and some of the details involved. She knows what happened to my brother, but she's sensitive enough not to raise the subject unless I do so first. There are few occasions on which I want to talk about what happened, and on those times, it's usually him I want to speak to about it all. No one else understands it in the way we do, and for that reason, we are forever connected.

I can sense from the way Andrew is still holding me that he doesn't believe me when I say I don't remember what the nightmare was about. Although I'm held close to him, his body feels tensed. He knows I'm lying to him. He must surely have noticed just how often his mother has mentioned my brother, and yet he never asks for more details than I've offered him. In fact, he doesn't ask much about my past at all. The subject of ex-boyfriends has remained off topic... the details of my childhood remain mine alone. Perhaps he prefers that what we share is untainted by our histories.

'We should try to go back to sleep,' he says, and he kisses my forehead in the dark, trying to ease me back into some state of restfulness.

Eventually, I fall back to sleep, but my dreams are unsettled, with strange bangs and nightmarish visions. When I wake for the second time, with my heart beating and my temperature soaring, Andrew is no longer in bed beside me. I sit up, expecting to see a glow from the en suite bathroom. But the room is thick with darkness. I lean over the side of the bed and fumble for my mobile phone on the carpet. I find it beneath the bed, and when I press the button on its side, its screen lights up: 3.37 a.m.

I shove the duvet back and get out of bed, and when I go to the door, which is pushed closed but not fully shut, I see a soft glow of lighting coming from downstairs. I hope I've not disturbed Andrew's night to the point that he hasn't been able to get back to sleep, although I wonder why, if that's the case, he hasn't just gone to bed in the spare room. I ease the door open gently, not wanting to disturb Rachel, just along the corridor. At the end of the landing, I stop when I hear voices coming from downstairs. Rachel's, and then Andrew's. I move on to the top step, treading carefully to avoid creaking the stairs. Like a child eavesdropping on her parents, I sit on the top step and crane my neck to try to hear what's being said.

'It's moving too fast,' I hear Rachel say.

'Everything's fine,' I hear Andrew say in reply. 'It's just you. You don't know when to back off.'

I feel a streak of irritability snake through me at the thought that they're discussing our relationship. I've known since I arrived here that Rachel resents me, and no matter what I've tried to do to improve the situation, she seems hellbent on assuming the worst of me, regardless. I want to hear Andrew speak in my defence, so I lean closer to the banister, desperate to hear what comes next.

'Are you in love with her?'

And then I hear Rachel laugh. Not a happy, *I'm so glad for you* kind of laugh, but a sneering, resentful scoff that attempts to belittle anything Andrew might feel for me. He's already told me he loves me, but I wait to hear his response to her anyway.

And that's when I lose my balance and almost fall headlong down the stairs. I grab at a spindle and steady myself, but I've already made too much noise. The kitchen falls into silence, and I swear under my breath before swinging my legs around so that I'm sideways on the step and out of view should anyone come to the kitchen doorway.

With my heart pounding, I wait to hear someone come into the hallway. There's no point in me trying to move now: I can't get off this staircase without making a noise, and if I try to make it look as though I've just got here and was on my way downstairs, it'll look far less suspicious than me trying to sneak back to the bedroom.

How easily I almost fell. Just a single mis-footing. Was this what happened last time, and not what I thought? Had Rachel not been there at all?

Andrew says something, but I don't catch what it is. And

then I hear Rachel say the same to him as she did to me on that evening that we went to the pub together: those same words that continued to ring in my ears far after the night was over.

'Don't fuck it up.'

THIRTY-ONE

The next morning, I leave before either Rachel or Andrew is up. He didn't come back to bed last night, and after I'd snuck back up to the bedroom, taking minutes to carefully cross just a few feet of landing, I heard him come up the stairs and go into the spare bedroom. Without having yet seen him, I get the sense that he's upset about something, and I can only hope that it's Rachel's words last night rather than the silence around my nightmare that has affected him enough to not return to me.

But what if it's not? There's a chance he may know more about my nightmare than I realise, that in sleep I might have revealed details I don't remember sharing. Maybe Rachel has filled in the gaps for him, though why would she care so much about my past? Despite her protestations at wanting to protect her son – that she would do *anything* for him – all she seems to be doing is standing in the way of his chance at happiness. What's the worst that could happen? If she knows about the accident and she tells Andrew what happened that day, I will talk to him about it. I will tell him the truth.

With nowhere else to go, I head back for the flat, with still two days until I'm officially locked out of what was once my home. I still have things there that I need to move out, though a lot of it could probably go to the tip or to the charity shop or could be left there to become Craig's problem to deal with. Condensed to just the necessary, my life's accumulations don't add up to much, though I suppose the same could be said for most people's existence. There's little that I need in the way of material things. I just want to feel wanted, and I know I'm not wanted at Andrew's house, not while Rachel is living there.

I get a text from him while I'm on the train, asking if I'm okay and saying he's sorry he missed me this morning. I don't reply. We had a lovely evening putting up the tree and decorating it together, but Rachel's shadow always seems to lurk over us, tainting everything. Though he chose me over her for the first time last night, I'm going to have to raise the subject of the overheard conversation between him and Rachel, and I don't feel ready for it yet. Nor do I want to do it over a text.

When I get to the flat, I'm relieved to find that my key still works in the front door. I'd half expected Craig to have changed the locks, just to make my life that little bit more difficult while I move my things out. Thankfully, even he has managed to avoid the temptation to be so petty. The flat reeks of damp. The smell catches in my throat as I head upstairs, and as predicted, it looks as though nothing has been done since I was last here.

Beneath the sink, I find a roll of black bags, and I tear one off and take it with me through to the bedroom. I start bagging up the remaining clothes that were left in the wardrobe, then I get another bag and begin on the piles of books stacked in the corner of the room, for which I never got around to buying a bookcase.

My phone starts ringing in my pocket. Andrew. I ignore it. Then a text pings through.

I'm outside.

I go to the window. His car is parked at the other side of the street, and Andrew is below the window, outside the front door. I sigh and go downstairs, letting him in and ushering him through the inside door before Craig can come out from the downstairs flat and find us here. I suspect I won't be back here on more than one other occasion, and if I miss him on both this and that, it would be perfect.

'How did you know I'd be here?'

'Educated guess.'

He follows me up to the flat.

'I'd offer you tea,' I say flatly. 'But I've no milk. Or water. Or,' I add, flicking a light switch, 'electricity, it would seem.'

'I don't want tea. I want you to come home. Have you left us?'

I can't look him in the eye, because I know where he's trying to go with this. He heard me last night on the stairs – or Rachel did – and he wants me to admit so.

'Us?'

'Me,' he quickly corrects himself.

'It's not my home,' I remind him.

He bites his lower lip. 'I know that. Stop being so pedantic. Look, Daisy... last night. What did you hear?'

'Not enough, and yet sufficient,' I mumble, passing him to go through to the living room. It occurs to me that I've no idea how I'm going to move the television. I can hardly prop it on my lap in the back of an Uber.

'What do you mean?'

I fold my arms across my chest. 'I heard your mother say that things are moving too fast between us, and I heard you tell her not to worry. Then I heard her tell you not to fuck things up. Funny... she said exactly the same thing to me in the pub.'

A smile plays out on Andrew's lips.

'What?' I ask. 'There's nothing funny about it. I told you... she hates me.'

'I'm not laughing. It's just ridiculous how different things can sound when they're taken out of context from the rest of a conversation.'

I wait, not sure what he's trying to get at. I heard what I heard, and I'm not sure what else it could have meant other than the obvious.

'Daisy, she doesn't hate you. She likes you. Why else would she be telling me not to fuck things up?'

'Why say that things are moving too fast then?'

'She's just being cautious for us, that's all. And she does have a tendency to project her past experiences on to things, but that's her problem. I'm not my dad.'

He steps closer to me and reaches out to put his hands on my shoulders. 'Daisy, I spoke to her again last night about what happened at dinner, with all the questions. She apologised for it. And then she told me to be careful that we didn't rush things, not to mess things up. If she didn't like you, she wouldn't be concerned about us either way, would she? But I understand why her behaviour has made you feel uncomfortable. I'll tell her she needs to go.'

'No,' I object, wondering where this sudden turn in attitude has come from. 'I don't want you to do that.' In truth, the thought is a tempting one, but it's not my place to make that decision. The more I think about what happened last night – how easily I might have fallen down that staircase, alone – the more I've begun to doubt Rachel's involvement in my previous fall. What if I've put two and two together and come up with fifty? She might resent me being in her son's life, but that doesn't equate a capacity for violence. It seems to me that keeping my enemy closer might be of greater benefit if I want things to work between Andrew and me. And if I want to give Rachel a real reason to hate me, getting Andrew to kick her out seems a perfect way to go about it.

'I know you haven't asked me to, but if it comes to it and I need to make a choice then there isn't one for me to make. I love you, Daisy. I know we've only known each other for a few months, but it's been more than enough. No one makes me happy in the way that you do.' He looks around at the state of the place. 'How long have you got to get your things out?'

'Until the end of tomorrow.'

In my pocket, my phone starts to ring again. When I take it out, Aisha's name lights up the screen.

'Do you mind if I take this?'

Andrew shakes his head, and I take the call.

'Daisy,' Aisha says, 'where are you?'

'At the flat. Is everything okay?'

My first thought is that something else has happened to her dada, and I hope to God it isn't true.

There's a pause at her end. 'I thought the flat was off limits?'

'I'm just collecting some of my stuff.'

Things haven't been right between Aisha and me for the past week or so. I know she thinks things with Andrew have moved too quickly, and she's not been shy in sharing her opinions. But now I suspect there's something more going on, and I'm starting to think she might be jealous. Whatever's going on with her, I hate this curtness between us.

'I need to see you.'

'Okay,' I say. 'What time are you in work tomorrow?'

'I don't really want this to wait until tomorrow. Can I meet you in town somewhere today?'

'In Ponty? Yeah, sure... as long as you don't mind coming here.'

'It's fine,' she says abruptly. 'Meet you in the Wetherspoons at about two-ish, is that okay?'

'Yeah, great,' I say, trying to sound casual while wondering what has happened. Aisha has never sounded so cold towards me. 'I'll see you at two.'

Andrew has been watching my end of the exchange, and he

questions me as I return my phone to my pocket. 'What was that all about?'

'Nothing. Just going to meet her for a drink. She's probably got news from work or something.'

'If you're meeting her at two o'clock, that gives me time to go and hire a van.'

'What about the car?'

'It'll be fine – I can leave it at the rental place, pick it up tomorrow.'

'But your mum—'

'Daisy,' he says, cutting me short. 'This isn't about her. Please. Let me help you. And then when you've found somewhere new to rent, I can move the stuff there. It's no big deal.' He puts his hands either side of my face and kisses me. 'Maybe I could let her keep the house and we could split the rent on the new place, what do you think?'

I smile and say nothing, not sure whether it's a joke or not. It's Andrew's house, after all, so I've no idea why he'd make a suggestion about moving. He's not the one who needs to leave.

THIRTY-TWO

There's a Wetherspoon's pub close to the train station in town, at the top end of the high street that's always quiet on weekday afternoons. When I go in through the main doors, I scan the countless rows of matching wooden tables, searching for Aisha's face among the mid-week drinkers and late lunch-breakers. I go to the back of the building, where there's a quiet family area, and there's Aisha, sitting with the handbag she'd loaned me in front of her on the table.

'Hey,' I say, sliding into the bench opposite her. 'Shall I get us a drink?'

'I'll get mine.'

She takes out her phone and scans the QR code on the menu for table service. I don't do the same. Her hostility towards me seems to have rendered me immobile.

'Has something happened?'

She completes her order before putting her phone down on the table and finally making eye contact with me. 'I don't know, Daisy. Has it?'

I sigh. I don't do cryptic, and I can't be bothered with

games. In all the years I've known and loved her, I've never seen this side of Aisha before; not with me, at least.

'I don't know what I've done,' I admit.

She reaches for the handbag I borrowed from her and opens an inside zip pocket. When she pulls something out from it, I'm unsure at first what I'm supposed to be looking at. Then the realisation hits me with the force of a punch. In her hand, Aisha holds a gold chain necklace with pearl pendant. I don't know much about jewellery, but I've had enough experience of covering in the department to know this single item is probably worth upwards of £400.

'I didn't take that,' I tell her softly, realising as I speak the words that this is exactly what an accused thief would say.

'I wish you hadn't given me the bag back,' she says, lowering her voice as she leans across the table. 'I'm handling stolen goods. Did you forget it was in there?'

She sits back and drops the necklace back into the bag, quickly zipping it back up. The barman comes over with a glass of orange juice, and she thanks him. I'm so stunned that I barely know what to say to her.

'You're my best friend. You don't really believe I'm capable of this?' I'm slapped across the face by the silence that follows. 'Christ, Aisha—'

'I know things haven't been easy for you recently. You've had money worries, and then the burst pipe at the flat, and—'

I feel my mouth dropping open like a stunned goldfish. 'Whenever things have been tough, I've worked more hours. Money's always been tight, but—'

'Probably not for much longer.'

Her words shut me silent for a moment. 'What's that supposed to mean?'

'Well, you've landed on your feet now, haven't you? Rich bloke with a fancy house… money won't be tight anymore.'

I feel tears pinch at the corners of my eyes, and I'm unsure whether I want to cry with anger or with hurt. 'If that's what you really think of me, and if that's why you think I'm with Andrew then why the hell would I need to steal a bloody necklace from my own workplace?'

My voice has risen, and I've attracted the attention of the barman who's now clearing coffee cups from a nearby table. I don't care. I can't believe that Aisha, the person I'm closest to more than anyone else in the world, can believe for even a second that I might be guilty of stealing.

'Then what's it doing in this bag?'

I sit back and press my head against the cushioned back of the bench. And as I do, the realisation falls from me, a weight dropped from the ceiling.

'Rachel.'

'What?'

'Rachel's done this,' I say, trying not to get overly animated. 'She commented on your bag the night I went for a drink with her, and I mentioned it being on loan from a friend at work. She planted it there knowing that at some point I'd return it to you.'

'Like she pushed you down the stairs?' Aisha's eyebrow rises in an arch. 'That would mean she'd have to have stolen this from the store, though? And then reported you for a theft she'd committed...'

She's looking at me sceptically, because I know it sounds ridiculous. But it's not entirely impossible, and while it's not impossible, there's a chance I could be right. It's the only thing that makes sense.

'Why would she do that?'

'She hates me.'

'So much so that she'd risk a criminal record?'

'Please, Aisha, I know it sounds insane. But there's something off about this woman – I've felt it since the first time I met her. You've known me for years... you can't believe this is me, not really.'

But Aisha says nothing, just looks at me as though I've let her down, and it's the worst feeling in the world. But I know I'm right. I don't know what that bitch is playing at, but I'm not going to let her win.

She sits back and tilts her head to the ceiling, unwilling to make eye contact with me. 'Don't you think there's something a bit "off" with more than just his mother?'

'What do you mean?'

'Andrew. Something just doesn't sit right.'

I'd known that Aisha was jealous of my new relationship. Beneath the banter about his good looks, there was an undercurrent of resentment that perhaps I'd just refused to acknowledge. Perhaps her failed date has added to her bitterness, but either way, any supposed concern she has about Andrew is unjustified.

'Like what?' I say defensively. 'He's done nothing but show me kindness and generosity.'

'Love-bombing, you mean.'

She looks at me now, challenging me.

'That's not it at all.'

'The fancy dinners… the print from the restaurant… it's all a bit much, don't you think?'

'I'm sorry you've not yet found someone who treats you well,' I tell her, and as soon as the words are spoken, I can't believe we're speaking to each other in this way. Aisha and I have never had a cross word between us. I wish now that I could swallow the statement back, so it had never been given oxygen to breathe.

'I care about you, Daisy. But something's not right. And I don't think it's just Rachel. There was a red flag that day you introduced us at the department store. I mean, come on… who speaks like that? *I understand you're the reason I'm able to take out young Daisy here.*'

'He never called me young.'

'Maybe not, but he still talked like he'd fallen out of an episode of *Bridgerton*.'

'Being well-spoken is a red flag now?'

Aisha puts her elbows on the table and rests her chin in her hands. 'You can't see it because you're in it, but something's not right. And if you really believe that Rachel has set you up with this stolen necklace, then why the hell would you stay in that situation?'

I say nothing, not knowing what the answer is. She's right... why would I stay? At the same time... where else do I go?

'You were defending him not so long ago,' I remind her. 'Wasn't it you who said I should forgive him for punching Craig? What happened to "defending my honour"?

Aisha looks unimpressed. 'I reconsidered,' she says blankly.

We sit in silence, both alone with our separate thoughts.

'What are you going to do?' I ask her.

Aisha's eyes look glassy, though I suspect it's more from anger than with tears.

'I don't know,' she admits.

'Please, Aisha,' I say. 'Please hide it somewhere. Just for the time being. I'm going to sort this all out, I promise. But please... I'm going to need your help.'

She runs a fingertip beneath her left eye, carefully saving the eyeliner that is as always so immaculately drawn.

'I'll get rid of it,' she tells me. 'But if you let me down, Daisy, I swear you and I will be done.'

THIRTY-THREE

When I get back to the flat, there's a van parked at the kerb outside the house. I'd left Andrew with the keys, and I find him upstairs, taking the television from the wall. Thankfully, it was nowhere near the wall where the pipe was burst, so I remain hopeful that this at least won't be water damaged. I can't afford to replace it, though being without a television isn't the worst thing in the world, not when I've got no home to put it in anyway.

'I thought you were staying away from DIY,' I say, as I round the corner into the living room.

'I assure you, I can be trusted with a screwdriver.'

'Just not an electric one, right?'

I'm trying my best to sound as breezy and casual as possible, because I'm not sure yet how best to approach the subject of Rachel and the accusation made against me at work. The woman has framed me for a crime. And not just any crime, but one that could cost me my job. I could get prosecuted. No one else will want to employ me if I end up with a criminal record, even if it is for something I didn't do.

I take a deep breath and will myself to think rationally. An accusation can't lead to prosecution without evidence. And as I'm innocent, there won't be any evidence.

But that doesn't change the fact that Rachel is a dangerous, vindictive bitch.

The thought that she has brought all this stress upon me makes me sick to my stomach. I had thought her resentful and bitter... now, I realise she's so much more than that.

'How did things go with Aisha?'

'Fine. It wasn't about work. She's having some problems at home.'

'Her granddad?'

'Yeah,' I say, remembering the unfair comment that Andrew had made last night about Aisha's relationship with her family. 'You got the van quickly,' I say, keen to change the subject.

'There's a place just off the A470, five minutes away. It was all straightforward.'

He manoeuvres the television past me and out on to the landing. When he goes downstairs with it, I go to the bedroom and watch him as he puts it into the back of the van. It's been years since I've felt so conflicted. Do I tell Andrew what I know and look for somewhere else to stay, or do I stay quiet about Rachel while I work out what she's playing at? Perhaps silence is a better plan, while I try to keep her on side.

I think of the planning and premeditation that went into first getting me suspended and then framing me, and I feel myself begin to heat up beneath my sweater. The way that woman has spoken to me – the way she's spoken to Andrew about me when she's thought I've not been around to hear anything. She has patronised and interrogated me; belittled me and insinuated that I'm not good enough for her precious bloody son.

Well, I am. And she may think she's got the better of me, but when it comes to it, we'll let Andrew show her which of us is really winning here.

By the time he comes back up to the flat, I'm almost shaking with anger. This isn't me, and I hate feeling this way. It must be so visible that Andrew takes one look at me and asks me what's happened. My voice shakes as I start to tell him, but I refuse to let that woman make me cry.

'It was Rachel,' I say, the words bursting from me like gunfire. 'Rachel made the allegation against me at work. She got me suspended. She stole that necklace from the jewellery department, and she planted it in a bag I'd borrowed from Aisha, and now Aisha's got the bag back and she thinks I'm a thief.'

'Whoa,' Andrew says, raising his hands. 'Slow down.'

I go through to the bedroom and sit on the bed, because the sofa is riddled with the damp that's been hanging in the air for all this time. Andrew follows me and sits beside me while I explain, slower this time, what happened with Aisha in the pub.

'Okay,' he says slowly, when I get to the end of events. I wait for him to say something else, but there's nothing.

'Is that it? Okay?'

'I'm thinking.'

I'm trying not to get frustrated by his silence, but it only makes things worse. 'For Christ's sake, Andrew, it's there in black and white. I'm not a bloody thief, but now even my best friend thinks I am.'

'Why?'

I turn sharply to him. 'Why? Because the set-up was convincing enough that—'

'No, I don't mean why does Aisha think you're a thief… I mean why would my mother do that to you?'

My heart is pounding with indignation, and yet when he speaks the question like that, the rationality of it is clear.

'It doesn't make sense, does it?' he adds.

'Maybe not to you, and certainly not to me, but we're not her, are we? I told you she hates me – I felt it almost straight away. There's always been an atmosphere between us. She pushed me down the stairs, and now she's going to cost me my job.'

A reaction flickers across Andrew's face, and I don't like what it implies. He thinks that if there has been an atmosphere, I'm the one who's responsible for it. And he still doesn't believe that she pushed me down the stairs.

'You've said before that you think she doesn't want you in the house,' he says, avoiding further conversation on my fall. 'So why would she then sabotage your job? Being suspended from work has meant you're there more often, and if she hates you, as you claim, why would she want that?'

Andrew's logical, calm approach to everything is usually something I admire. Today, when the subject is Rachel, all it does is manage to rankle me further.

'Why do you always do this? You always defend her, even when it's obvious she's at fault! It's like the woman can do no bloody wrong.' I pause and take a deep breath. 'Have you ever heard of enmeshment?'

'No. Please... enlighten me.'

'Google it.' I get up and leave the room, grabbing some of the last of my things from the landing. Outside, it has started to rain. I stand in the open front doorway as fat drops slap against the house, sliding down the front windowpane like tears. The more I go over Andrew's words, the more sense they start to make, and yet Rachel's guilt still looms over me like a cloud, threatening to assault me with a downpour.

Because while Andrew's words may seem logical, there is no other explanation than that Rachel has done this to me.

I sense Andrew behind me, but don't turn to him. 'Do you still want me to help you clear out your stuff?' he asks.

The bags in my hand weigh me down with their emptiness. I could throw their contents in a skip and not miss any of it. 'I don't seem to have much choice, do I?'

'You always have a choice, Daisy.'

I appreciate the sentiment, although I'm not sure it's true. Sensing my doubts, Andrew puts his arms around me. 'I'll help you get to the bottom of this allegation,' he says, turning me towards him. 'I don't believe that my mother's involved, but I can speak to her about the bag if you'd like me to.'

'No,' I say quickly. 'Please. Don't say anything to her. I need to sort this out myself.'

Andrew kisses the top of my head before going back up to the flat. I realise I'm not alone, and sense Craig before I see him, the door to his flat ajar this whole time. It eases open and he stands leaning against the doorframe, his arms folded across his chest. I wonder just how much of the conversation he overheard.

With a smug smile, Craig looks me up and down, his gaze making me feel exposed.

'You should air your dirty laundry behind closed doors,' he says. 'You never know who might be listening in.'

THIRTY-FOUR

I wait until the following evening for a time when both Andrew and Rachel aren't home. She's gone out with a friend, and Andrew is working late after a conference in Cardiff. I spent the last twenty-four hours trying to avoid Rachel, making polite small talk whenever we were in the same room, but trying as much as possible to be out of the house. I spent today at the local library, researching my rights in this situation with work and contacting Citizen's Advice to see what I'm able to do. The advice was unhelpful; until the 'investigation' has taken place, there's little I can do. Sitting tight and being patient has never been something I'm good at, so as soon as Rachel's left for her night out, I start my search to prove her guilt.

In the living room, there's a coffee table that has storage within it, and a sideboard with three drawers and cupboards. I start with the table, but there's nothing inside other than a few books, a supermarket groceries receipt, and an elastic hairband. I realise I've never had a need to look in the sideboard before, so I'm not sure what Andrew keeps in there. Back in the flat, the unit beneath my television had been crammed with old DVDs of no use to anyone anymore, electrical cables that fitted with nothing, old greetings cards I couldn't bring myself to recycle, and all the miscellaneous junk that I imagine is stored in the sideboards of most homes: tea lights and batteries and coasters and packs of playing cards, and those little screwdrivers that come in Christmas crackers that people keep for 'just in case'.

Yet in Andrew's sideboard, there is next to nothing. In the right-hand drawer, there's a phone charger, a set of coasters that haven't been taken out of their display box, a letter addressed to Andrew from a car rental company, a roll of Sellotape and an Amazon gift card. The other drawers are empty, as are the cupboards.

Where is all Andrew's *stuff*? The day-to-day stuff that accumulates through the simple act of living; the things people resolve to declutter their lives of, yet never seem to have time to do? I suppose there are people who embrace a minimalist lifestyle and manage to achieve it, and it's easier to do now, with so much paperwork and documentation sent and stored online.

In the kitchen, the cupboards store the bare minimum required for cooking. There are utensils and crockery, pots and pans, but again, there are none of the excess items that accumulate in so many people's homes. Whenever Aisha used to go into one of my kitchen cupboards for a mug or the pot where I kept the tea bags, I would always find myself apologising for the state of them, and the way in which eight times out of ten, a jar or a tin would fly out from the opened door, launched from the overload like a missile being fired by an undercover assassin.

The pain that grips my heart is sudden and tight. My home is gone. My best friend is gone. Life as I've known it for these past few years has been ripped out from under me, and I wasn't prepared for it to happen again. I may have lost the flat, I tell myself, but I refuse to lose Aisha too. And there's no way I'm losing Andrew. Regardless of how insidious Rachel is, when I'm with her son, I'm the happiest I've been in years. I just need to find a way to get her out of the picture.

The narrow table in the hallway holds nothing of any interest, nor does the utility room or the cupboard beneath the stairs where the ironing board and vacuum cleaner are stored. I don't know what I'm hoping to find, but there must be *something*. Something that proves I'm right in my feeling about there just being something 'off' about Rachel.

When I'm finished downstairs, I head to the bedrooms, aware that I'm running out of time. I start with Rachel's. In her wardrobe full of beautiful items, I search pockets for receipts or notes or... anything. I am desperate. And until this moment, perhaps I hadn't realised just how desperate I am.

I sit on the pink silk duvet and scan the room as my heart races with a growing sense of panic. It is again minimalist in here, with just a bed, wardrobe and bedside tables, and the soft furnishings are also kept to a minimum. Rachel's stay is temporary though, so there wouldn't be any point in her decorating the place to suit her tastes. Not unless she was planning on her living here becoming something more permanent.

In the bedside drawer, I find make-up bags and hair styling tools. I'm not sure what makes me open the bags, and I'm expecting to find nothing more than brushes and tubes, pots and powders. But in one, I find something else. A passport tucked inside an inner pocket.

Of course, Rachel looks beautiful in her passport photograph. While the rest of us mere mortals have one eye bigger than the other, making it look as though we're giving the camera a cheeky wink, or we've taken the 'no smile' rule to an extreme that results in the appearance of a serial killer's police mugshot, Rachel's image is a *Vogue* front cover, complete with smoky eye make-up and perfectly styled beach waves. I wonder how old the passport might be, and how soon it might expire. She looks so young in the photograph, as fresh-faced and flawless as had the image been filtered.

But while I'm searching for an expiry date, it's another detail that catches my eye.

Rachel Leanne Miller

13.07.80

13th July 1980

Her birthday is in July. But that can't be right. Andrew was buying her a birthday present in October. The perfume was a birthday present... wasn't it? I'm sure that's what he'd said. The details of that day are imprinted on my memory. It wasn't a Christmas present; she'd been wearing the perfume when I'd first met her, and that was still in October.

But why lie about something as innocuous as a birthday month?

Then I realise it's not just the month.

1980... that would make Rachel forty-five. But I've been led to believe that she's fifty-four. I've never been explicitly told so – there's never been a reason why her age might have come up in conversation – but at some point, I'd made the link between Andrew being thirty-nine and Rachel having had him at fifteen. That would make her fifty-four. Yet her passport very clearly claims something else.

I can't understand why either of them would have lied about her date of birth. People tend to shave years off, not add them on. It makes no sense, with no gain to be won from it. And if Rachel has lied about her age, that means Andrew has lied to me about his.

It's as I sit back on the bed that I notice it. The black overnight bag that's shoved on the narrow shelf inside the top of the wardrobe, strangely messy-looking amid the order of Rachel's personal space. Yet it's not the bag that catches my eye. It's what inside it. From beyond the slightly opened zip, I see a flash of blue. It is familiar in the kind of way that grips at a memory, plucking it from the obscurity of my subconscious and planting me firmly in a different time and place. But it's not a time or place of which I want to be reminded or to which I would ever long to return.

I get up and stand on the end of Rachel's bed to reach the top shelf of the tall wardrobe. The bag almost falls out on me when I pull at it, and as I place it on the duvet with shaking hands, I already know what I'm about to find.

Blue leather-look material, with a ridged pattern along the seams. The long chain handle that always used to click annoyingly against the chunky metal buttons of my winter coat.

The bag that was stolen from me on the evening I was mugged. On the same day that I first met Andrew.

THIRTY-FIVE

I need to get out of here. While I'm in this house, surrounded by Andrew and by Rachel, I can't think properly. I shouldn't have come back here yesterday, after Aisha had tried to warn me. Because that's what she was doing... I realise that now. I'd thought yesterday that she was simply jealous, and that her animosity towards Andrew was merely a reflection of that. Now, I'm not so sure. Nothing makes sense. This bag makes no sense.

I need to leave. I need to work out what I'm going to do, but I can't do that here. I'm just going to have to face the expense of the Travelodge again, and hope that over the next few days I'm able to sort out the mix-up at work and clear my name. Perhaps I did the wrong thing by asking Aisha to get rid of that necklace. If I'd returned it, surely they would believe in my innocence? No one would steal from their workplace to then return the stolen item weeks later.

Mix-up, I think bitterly. Yeah, right. My God... it seems Rachel is responsible for so much more than getting me suspended from my job.

In the spare room that I was encouraged to think of as mine, I hurriedly pack the bare minimum I'll need into a rucksack and a shoulder bag. All my things from the flat are now in Andrew's garage, but it occurs to me that even if I never saw all that stuff again, it wouldn't be the end of the world. They're just things. Above all else, I need to protect my sanity, and I can't do that while I'm still under the same roof as that woman. She has lied about everything. But even worse is the thought that perhaps so has Andrew.

I'm going to have to start again, from scratch. Yet it won't be the first time my life has required a completely new beginning.

I call Aisha, but it rings through to answerphone. She doesn't want to speak to me, and the thought that she still believes me guilty is crushing. If Aisha doesn't believe my innocence, then it's unlikely anyone else will. And while there's no one else to help me, I'll just have to take care of myself, as I've always done. I would have just loved to have heard her voice. To have been able to speak to someone I know I can trust.

I need to speak to you – can you call me when you get this? You were right to be concerned about me. I'm sorry for everything x

I send the text and go downstairs, where I plan to order an Uber. They usually arrive within minutes, and with Rachel and Andrew both out, I have plenty of time to be gone from here before either of them gets home. I don't know why they've lied. I don't know why my stolen handbag is in her bedroom. I'm not sure I even want to hear the reasons – or excuses – for any of it.

I've not yet made the Uber booking when the front door opens. Rachel stands in the doorway looking glamorous as ever, a sequinned top shimmering beneath her tailored winter coat.

'I thought you were on a night out,' I say, hearing the guilt in my words, as though I'm the one who's done something wrong.

'I was supposed to be,' she says, slipping her heeled boots from her feet and hanging her bag on one of the coat hooks, 'but I've got this terrible headache. I was hoping it would ease up, but it's getting worse.' She glances at the bags at the foot of the staircase. 'Were you off out somewhere?'

'No,' I say too hurriedly. 'I just... I was bringing some of my things in from the garage.'

I take my coat off, feeling my heart sink. I wanted to get out of here tonight. Perhaps I can still do that, after she's gone to bed. Or perhaps I could suggest she has a bath, to help her headache, and I can sneak out then. Maybe I could make her a warm drink and lace it with something to make her fall asleep. My God... what has happened to me? I suppose when you're in someone's company for long enough, it's easy enough to develop their traits.

Whatever you do, I tell myself, just don't let her know anything's wrong. If she thinks that everything is as it was this morning, there'll be no reason to find out how she might possibly react to learning otherwise.

'Why don't I make you a cup of tea and get you some paracetamol?' I suggest.

'Would you mind?'

'Of course not. You go into the living room... I'll bring them through in a minute.'

I go down to the kitchen, my heart pounding. I don't know what to think. I don't know what to do. I just need to get away from her.

I prolong the task of making a cup of tea, taking my time while I try to organise my thoughts. But I can't seem to put them into any kind of order. All I keep coming back to is the thought of Andrew lying to me. Rachel... yes. It doesn't surprise me. I already knew she hated me, although I was unaware of the extremity of that feeling. But Andrew...

I'd believed him when he'd told me he loved me, and that makes everything so much worse.

I take the tea and a packet of tablets through to the living room, where Rachel is sitting on the sofa. The woman never seems to relax. Even now, apparently with a raging headache, she is sitting at the edge of the sofa, back straight, hands on her knees, like someone waiting to be invited into an interview room.

The headache is probably a lie, I remind myself – much the same as everything that comes out of this woman's mouth.

'Take two of these,' I say, passing her the packet.

The front door is opened. A moment later, Andrew appears in the living room doorway.

'Hey,' he says, dropping his shoulder bag on the floor before taking off his coat. 'My two favourite women.'

He comes to me and plants a kiss on my forehead, and I feel the weight of Rachel's gaze as she watches us together. I wonder if she notices the way my body tenses when he nears me. I wonder whether he senses that I would rather be anywhere than here, and that if I was able to, I would shove his hands away from mine and tell him to stay the hell away from me. But I can do neither of these things, not while I have no idea what either of these people might be capable of.

I have never felt more claustrophobic in my life. I have never felt more trapped.

'Is everything okay?' he asks me, his eyebrows furrowing with feigned concern. 'You look as though you're coming down with something.'

The handsome face looks so different now, beneath the brightness of his lies. The kind eyes seem territorial. This man might once have been a drug, but I'm not so addicted that I don't know when I've had enough of a good thing.

Could Rachel possibly have that bag without Andrew

knowing anything about it? Maybe. She's the one who's proved herself unreliable... not him.

'I think I might be,' I say, moving away from them both. 'If you don't mind, I think I'll have an early night. I hope your headache goes soon, Rachel.'

THIRTY-SIX

When Andrew comes into the bedroom, I pretend to be asleep. I'm lying on my side, facing away from him, and when I sense him approach the end of the bed, I fear for a moment that he might come around to check whether I really am sleeping. He must realise that by coming to bed in the spare room rather than in his, I'd prefer to be alone tonight. I wait for the sounds of him undressing to get into bed, grateful when he doesn't, and by the time he leaves the room, I've been holding my breath for an uncomfortable amount of time.

The most terrifying thoughts have been tormenting me since I came upstairs hours ago. I keep going over the evening of the mugging, reliving those moments when I was assaulted. It wasn't Rachel or Andrew; despite not having seen my attacker's face, I am certain that it couldn't have been. Andrew is far taller than the boy who stole my bag, and I'm pretty sure it was a boy rather than a man, someone not yet out of his teens. It wasn't a woman, so it couldn't have been Rachel.

And yet your stolen bag was in her room, I remind myself. And the fact that it wasn't either of them in person doesn't mean neither was responsible for orchestrating the attack.

Rachel. This is exactly the kind of thing I now know her to be capable of. But why?

I can't lie here until the morning, waiting for a good time to leave. There is never going to be a right time. The time is now.

I wait to hear Andrew go down the landing, but he doesn't. Instead, he goes back downstairs. I check my phone for the time. It is twenty minutes past midnight. I realise Aisha still hasn't replied to my text. Why is Andrew going back downstairs? Why doesn't he just go to bed? With him downstairs, getting out of the house is going to be so much more difficult.

I slide from beneath the duvet. I'd changed into pyjamas in case Andrew got into bed beside me. It would have looked suspicious if he'd found me fully dressed, as I'd originally intended to stay. It is cold tonight, the chilly temperature of the bedroom hitting me as I place my bare feet on the carpet. The clothes I wore yesterday are folded in a pile on the bedside table. I dress slowly, careful not to make a sound. My things are already packed in the bag I brought back to the bedroom with me after Rachel had seen it last night. If Andrew had noticed it when he came home, he made no mention of it.

I put on some extra layers and try to work out where I left my coat. Shit... it's in the living room. If that's where Andrew is, I'm just going to leave without it. I only need to get into a taxi, and the taxi can drop me off at a hotel somewhere. I can pick up another coat from somewhere tomorrow.

Trying to avoid further deliberation, I take my bag with me out on to the landing. At the top of the stairs, between the slats of the banister, the soft glow of lamplight comes from the living room. The television is on; I can make out the low sounds of voices arguing. I step on to the top of the staircase, wincing as it creaks beneath my feet. There is movement at the living room doorway that stops me in my tracks.

Through the open doorway, I can see the end of one of the sofas: the one that has the seascape print hanging behind it.

There is movement again, a swish of Rachel's long blonde hair before I see her face in a side profile as her head lolls back on to one of the cushions. It is the most relaxed I have ever seen her. The happiest she has ever looked. I grip the banister as I move to descend another step, but I stop when I see Andrew. He is above her, leaning over her. He moves back, out of view for a moment. I hear the tinkle of Rachel's tapped-glass laughter, and then another noise. A zip being undone. My heart stops. My tongue swells like a sponge.

Rachel moans softly. I taste bile in my mouth.

When he reappears, I watch as Andrew moves over Rachel again, their faces inches apart, his hand in her loose hair, gripping her closely as he has done so many times to me. My own hand moves to my mouth, the bile turning to sickness in my throat as I watch them kiss like lovers.

THIRTY-SEVEN

Three hours later, Andrew and Rachel finally come upstairs. I've no idea whether they go to their own rooms or whether they go to one together, and I don't care. I'm assuming that after what I'd seen, they'd fallen asleep on the sofa. Either that, or they've been down there all this time, chatting and laughing... doing things too disgusting to think about. Behaving as though everything is normal.

I couldn't leave. There was no way of getting down the stairs and to the front door without at least one of them hearing me, and if they had and they'd tried to stop me, what would have happened then? Against one of them, I might have stood a chance, but with both here, I would have been trapped. I couldn't risk it, so I was forced to come back upstairs and wait it out, sitting in the spare room all this time while thoughts of them together filled my head in visions that were sickening and grotesque.

Everything is a lie. Everything.

For the last three hours I have sat on the bed in the darkness and waited. I watched the door, praying that it wouldn't open and that I wouldn't be faced with Andrew, because I know I won't be able to conceal what I saw. It has repulsed me. They are sick. I'd accused him of being enmeshed with his mother, but this... I can't even find the words for it. I don't want to hear their excuses. I don't want to listen to any more of their lies.

After they come upstairs, I wait an hour longer. I need for them to be asleep when I leave; not just in the light kind of slumber that comes soon after drifting off but rather fully immersed in a deep sleep that won't be disturbed by the creaking of a stair or the clicking of the front door. I haven't been able to cry. The fear of what might happen after this is keeping me from tears, my body seeming to reserve its energies for when they may be more greatly needed.

By the time 5.15 a.m. arrives, I've ordered an Uber. I've messaged Aisha again, asking if she's awake, but the WhatsApp message hasn't yet gained a double tick to say it's been received. In a way, perhaps it's better that she didn't get the message; I'd rather that than have her read it and ignore me. I don't know what I'd planned to tell her if she'd replied. *I've just seen my boyfriend with his tongue in his mother's mouth.* Not really a fair way to tear someone from their sleep.

I take my overnight bag, and the rucksack crammed with clothing, toiletries and make-up downstairs. It takes minutes just to cross the landing and then get down the staircase, edging my way against the walls like some kind of unconvincing ninja. In the hallway, I rest my things by the front door and slip on my coat, retrieved from the living room, and trainers, glancing every now and then at my phone to check the location of the Uber. It's only a couple of minutes away.

And then the bloody thing starts ringing. I swipe it from the hallway table and answer quickly, not recognising the number. Beneath my coat, my heart races with the notion that the noise has probably just woken Andrew or Rachel. Or both.

'Daisy?'

'Hello,' I whisper, moving into the living room and gently pushing the door closed behind me. 'Who's this?'

'Daisy, it's Parveen.'

I don't think Aisha's nana has ever called me before. I wasn't even aware she had my number. Why is she ringing me now, at not yet even 6 a.m.?

'Oh, hi. Everything okay?'

'I need to get hold of Aisha. Her phone keeps going straight to answerphone. Is she there with you? She texted me last night to say she was staying at your flat.'

My skin raises with goosebumps.

'No. No, she's not with me.' And why would Aisha have told her nana that? She knows the state the flat is in, and she knows I'm no longer living there. Why would she lie to her Nana about where she would be?

My phone bleeps in my ear and I move it from my head. The Uber is outside waiting for me. 'Parveen, I'm going to have to call you back, can you give me two minutes?'

'Okay. But I need to get hold of Aisha as soon as possible. It's her dada... he's had another stroke.'

I press my fingers to my forehead. 'Oh no. I'm so sorry. Look... I'll call you right back, okay?'

I end the call. Bile rests in my throat. Aisha doesn't lie to her grandparents; she has no need to. And I don't believe for a second that she would have told her nana she'd be staying with me, not while things are so frosty between us. She'll want to know what's happened to her dada, and she'll want to get to him as quickly as possible.

So, where on earth is she?

My phone starts ringing and I flick it to silent before answering. 'I'm coming out now,' I tell the Uber driver. But when I open the living room door, Andrew is standing at the other side of it.

'Are you going somewhere?' he asks, gesturing to the bags.

My pulse is racing. The sweat and panic I can feel trickling down my spine must surely be visible. I need to get out of here, but I know Andrew isn't going to let it be easy for me.

He looks at me with a face I know so well, yet I realise I don't really know him at all. Is he going to try to stop me leaving this house? I lower my phone from the side of the head. The Uber driver has already cut off the call. Now, I wish I'd asked him to stay on the line.

'I'm going to check into a hotel for a few nights.' I nearly mention needing to find Aisha, but I stop myself. He doesn't need to know that, and I don't want him to offer his help.

'Has something happened?'

My heart is beating so hard now it's making me feel sick. Does he really not know what I saw last night? Or is he aware, and this is all part of some warped gaslighting manoeuvre aimed at making me doubt myself? Either way, I don't have the time to be standing here.

'I've got to go.' I step towards him, but he puts his hands on my shoulders, stopping me from passing.

'Daisy, please, I don't understand—'

'Who is she, Andrew? Because if Rachel's your mother, then what I saw last night is beyond fucked up.'

There is barely a flicker of a reaction on his face. It's almost as though he already knew what I'd seen. Almost as though they had meant for me to see it.

I feel his hands tighten on my shoulders.

'There's a taxi waiting outside for me. Are you going to try to stop me from leaving?'

And for an awful second, I think he might. The craziest images flood my head: being dragged into the kitchen screaming; or worse, unconscious, with no one knowing where I am. Because I am isolated here, vulnerable to a person I stupidly, naïvely trusted at the cost of all else.

He glances to the staircase. 'No. I'm not going to stop you.'

His hands fall from my shoulders, and he steps away, allowing me to leave.

This should be the point at which I do so. I should grab my bags and rush straight through the front door; I should forget what I saw and leave this house without ever thinking of either of these people again. But I know I won't be able to do that. And I deserve an answer.

'Who is she, Andrew?'

He looks me in the eye, unflinching, so brazen that for a moment the words seem to echo as though they've not been spoken at all and have merely come from inside my own head, an imagining of the worst outcome my brain can conjure.

'Rachel is my wife.'

THIRTY-EIGHT

In the Uber, my hands shake uncontrollably as I call Aisha's nana back and ask her where she is. All my energy is being thrown towards her and her family, because if I think for longer than a moment of the people I've just left behind, I'm afraid it might break, and what use will I be to my friend then? Parveen tells me that she's in the Heath hospital with her husband. I tell her not to worry about trying to get hold of Aisha as I'll do it for her, but even as I say the words, a sinking feeling hangs in my chest. I feel as though I'm making a promise I have no guarantee of keeping. Something is wrong. I don't know what, but I just get the sense that something has happened to Aisha. And I can't shake off the feeling that whatever has happened, it has something to do with me.

I try her phone again. It goes straight to answerphone.

Thoughts of Aisha are keeping me from dwelling on others of Andrew and Rachel, though I'd give anything for my doubts to be confirmed wrong. My brain spirals into a series of possible scenarios, none of which have happy endings. I keep glancing at my phone as though her name might appear at any moment, and the whole thing has been some kind of mix-up. A broken phone. A miscommunication.

Rachel is my wife.

What kind of sick, twisted game has this couple been playing for all this time?

'Can you take me to the police station?' I ask the driver, yanking myself from thoughts of Andrew and Rachel.

'Bridgend?'

'Yes, please.'

Thankfully, the journey to the station is short. As I enter the reception area, I get a strange look from the desk sergeant, who eyes my baggage suspiciously, as though I'm an all-night drinker who's confused about my whereabouts and is about to try to check in to an en suite room.

'My friend is missing,' I tell him, dumping my bags at my feet. 'I think something's happened to her.'

I give him the details and the name of her next of kin. Then he asks why, if her family think she's missing, none of them has reported it already. I explain that her grandmother is in hospital with her grandfather, who's suffered a stroke, and that she was under the impression that Aisha was staying at my place.

'So when would your friend have last been seen?' the officer asks.

'Whatever time she finished work yesterday, I'm guessing.'

'And what sort of time would that have been?'

'I don't know. Depends whether she was on a late shift. Anywhere between four and ten p.m.'

The officer rubs his chin. 'So, potentially, she's been seen by colleagues within the last ten hours. And she's—' He stops to scan the notes he's taken while I gave him Aisha's details. 'Thirty years old.' He raises an eyebrow, letting the left caterpillar finish his point for him.

'I know it might seem like worrying unnecessarily, but there's no way Aisha would have told her grandmother she was staying at my flat. I've been evicted from there. She would never have said—'

'She would never have said,' the officer repeats, when I abandon my sentence midway through. 'What?'

But my brain is working faster than any words will be able to keep up. What if Aisha had never told her nana she was staying with me? Until now, I've assumed the words were spoken. But what if they'd been sent? That might have been the message Nana had received, but it doesn't mean that Aisha was the one to have written or sent it.

'Oh God,' I say. 'I think this might be all my fault.'

The desk sergeant glances at his phone to check the time.

'Please,' I say, his lack of interest now tangible. 'I know this is confusing but hear me out.'

I tell him about Rachel and how odd she's been with me since I met Andrew. I give him details about my suspension from work, the stolen necklace in the handbag, and asking Aisha to help me prove my innocence. Then I tell him about the passport details and the stolen bag I found in her bedroom. Finally, I tell him about seeing Andrew and Rachel together last night.

'Okay,' he says casually, as though I've just run off details of the local train timetable. 'And how do you think this might relate to your friend?'

'I asked for her help,' I say, getting frustrated at having to repeat myself. 'Rachel and Andrew... they're not who I thought they were. I found her passport in the house. Her birthday is in July, so why was Andrew buying her a birthday present when I met him in October?

'Always best to be organised,' the man says with a shrug.

'Why lie about her age?' I press, not in the mood for attempts at humour.

'A woman lying about her age isn't a criminal offence.'

'No,' I say through gritted teeth. 'But duping someone into a relationship and pretending your wife is your mother must surely be illegal in some way, mustn't it?'

The man's nose wrinkles in disgust, and I'm sure that for a millisecond a smirk plays out on his lips. He thinks I'm crazy, or that I'm some vengeful ex plotting the kind of fabrication that would have a soap writer rubbing his hands with thoughts of a Christmas special. And he sure as hell can't see how any of this relates to Aisha being missing.

The truth is, neither can I. But I know I can't ignore the possibility.

'You thought she was his mother?' the officer confirms with a raised eyebrow. I can imagine him later, sharing the story with his colleagues while they're clocking off from their shift. Laughing at just how stupid some people can be.

'Can you try the local hospitals or something?' I ask, my voice growing desperate. 'We're wasting time.'

'I'll speak to my superior.'

'Great.' I grab my bags. I'll be better off trying to find Aisha myself, which is exactly what I intend to do.

THIRTY-NINE

Having hailed a taxi, the first number I try is the hospital where Aisha's grandfather has been taken. If it's the case that she's been hurt in some way or had some kind of accident, the best possible outcome will be that she's there, with her grandparents already in the same building.

'Hi, I wonder if you could help me. I'm looking for a friend who's gone missing. Her name is Aisha Shah. She's thirty, she has long dark hair... she wears black a lot of the time, and a lot of eyeliner. I—'

'Could I please take some details from you?' the robotic female voice at the other end of the call says.

'I'm giving you details. Are you taking them down?'

'What's your name please, caller?'

'Daisy. Daisy White.'

'Are you a relative?'

'No, but—'

'I'm afraid I can't give you any information relating to patients unless you're a relative.'

'Her grandparents are both already at the hospital,' I

explain. 'Parveen and Yousuf Shah. He was brought in last night after a stroke.'

'I'm afraid I can't give you any information relating to patients unless you're a relative,' the woman repeats, word for word, like a soulless television presenter reading badly from a cue card.

I mutter an obscenity beneath my breath, frustrated at the time that's being wasted. Time that we don't have. Time that Aisha may not have.

I make another two calls to local hospitals, and on the second, to Llandough hospital, I get someone who talks to me with the empathy and compassion of a human being rather than with the monotonous drone of a machine.

'She has a scar above her right eyebrow, almost V-shaped,' I tell the woman, having already given Aisha's personal details. 'She got it when she was child… her cousin tripped her over when they were at the beach, and she hit her face on a rock. I know you're not supposed to tell me anything, but please… I just want to know where she is. I think something might have happened to her.'

'Could you give me a few minutes? Just hold the line, okay?'

I wait for what feels an eternity. We are stuck in morning traffic now, in a stream of vehicles making their way towards the M4.

'Do you want me to carry on towards the Heath?' the driver asks, having presumably heard the details of my end of the conversation. I've done nothing to hide them, so he hasn't been able to help but overhear.

'Yes please.' I'll need to get Parveen and take her with me to the other hospital, if it turns out that Aisha is there. It's the only way I'll be allowed access to her.

'Hello?'

'Oh, hi,' I say, returning my focus to the call. 'Thanks for coming back to me. Is she there… have you found her?'

'All I'm able to say is, you might be better off coming to the hospital in person.'

My heart twists with a mixture of relief and panic. Aisha is there. This woman isn't allowed to tell me so, but she's doing it without saying the words.

'Okay. Thank you... thank you so much. I'm on my way.'

I don't ask how she is or what has happened. There's no point; the woman won't be able to tell me anything. She's probably done more than she should just by letting me know that Aisha is there.

I end the call and phone Parveen, but she doesn't answer.

'Parveen,' I say to the answerphone. 'It's Daisy. I've found Aisha. I'm coming to pick you up in a taxi... I can take you to her. Just let me know you've got this and let me know where to meet you when I get there. I'll be about half an hour.'

If the traffic ever starts moving, I think. I stare at the stationary stream of cars that lies ahead of us. It'll probably take longer to get to Aisha's nana than I've just said, and then it'll probably be the same again to Llandough, through the morning rush hour.

I just hope that by the time we get there, we won't be too late.

FORTY

As we're pulling off the bypass that runs alongside the Heath hospital a little over half an hour later, a text pings through on my phone. It's from Parveen.

Waiting at the double doors at block D

'I can't get down there,' the taxi driver says when I give him the directions. 'That end of the hospital is under construction. Can you ask her to meet us at the entrance of C block?'

'Is that where the X-ray unit is?' I'd once had to come here after my brother had broken his wrist playing rugby.

'Yeah.'

I know the hospital grounds well enough to know the basic layout. To get to the entrance of C block from where she'll be waiting for me, Parveen would have to walk back through the maternity unit and A&E. It'd be quicker for me to cut through to the D block doors on foot and bring her back to meet the driver here. I explain my idea to him, and he pulls over by a row of bollards.

'I won't be long.'

He says nothing. I've not even looked at the metre; I don't dare.

I'll be two minutes, I text back.

As I cut across the car park and turn a corner where a JCB blocks the road, I see this whole end of the hospital is covered with scaffolding. Sections of the car park have been cordoned off, and there are signs redirecting pedestrians from the area I'm approaching. Ignoring them, I make my way to the entrance to block D, which is around a further two corners, the double doors facing the brick wall of another wing of the building. For a place with so much scaffolding and machinery, there are surprisingly few workers. I pass a man in a high-vis jacket standing by a road digger, but he's too engrossed in the argument he's having with whoever's at the other end of his mobile call to bother to tell me I need to turn around and head back the way I came. If he's still here on the way back, I'm guessing it'll be easier to garner sympathy once I've got Aisha's nana on my arm, and I've always found that in moments of uncertainty, it's sometimes useful to just play ignorant.

I turn a final corner to see the entranceway to my right. The path that runs between the two sections of building is littered with cigarette ends and drinks cans, despite the bin that's placed right by the electric doors. When I reach them, Nana isn't here. I go inside and scan the empty corridor, the place deserted. I try her mobile. The signal is weak inside the hospital, so I go outside to try again.

'Parveen,' I say, when it goes straight to answerphone, 'I'm at D block, like we arranged. Can you let me know where you are when you get this?'

I turn to go back inside the building, where there's a row of plastic chairs screwed to the floor near the lifts. But I don't make it. A blow to the head sends me flying, and I feel a second hit when my head bounces from the brick wall of the opposite hospital wing. When I turn, the blood running into my eye distorts my vision. And then everything fades to black as something is thrown over my head.

Arms close around me. I try to fight back, but the two blows to the head have left me so disoriented that I barely have the strength to hold up my own weight.

'Calm down,' a voice says, distant and detached.

I kick and struggle, but inside the darkness, the world is slipping away from me. I can feel my body weakening from my head down, my arms becoming weaker as the force around them grows; my legs turning to marshmallow as I'm dragged across the concrete.

Someone will come, I keep telling myself. Someone will see something.

But no one comes. And as I'm thrown like a bin bag full of rubbish on to a hard, cold floor, the voice moves closer for a moment, before I begin to lose consciousness.

'Just think… it won't be long before you get to see your brother again.'

FORTY-ONE

Liam isn't expecting to see me today. There's a flicker of a reaction at his left eye, and I wonder whether it's surprise or disappointment. Perhaps there's an element of both. He's in the upstairs day room when I arrive. There are three patients in the room, but no communication between any of them. A television is on in the corner, filling the silence with the chatter of a panel of women discussing the possibility that washing powder might be affecting people's libido.

'Hi Liam,' I say, crouching beside his wheelchair so that I'm nearer to his height. 'Shall we go down to your room?'

I'm not expecting him to respond, but he does. A single blink. Yes.

I stand and take hold of the wheelchair's handles, manoeuvring it in a three-point turn before pushing Liam from the day room and into the corridor. In his room, the light and the radio have both been left on. I turn them off and push his chair over to the window before pulling the visitor's chair alongside him.

'I've done it,' I say, putting my hand over his. His fingers are cold and without response. I know he's still angry with me, but everything I've done, I've done for him.

'Ooh, hello.' Kathleen bustles into the room, as smiley as ever. It isn't possible that she can always be this happy. I wonder what she's like at home. She's probably a terrible wife, or a useless mother. Perhaps she collects thimbles from around the world, or maybe she's the kind of demonic person who tears off foil in a way that leaves half the roll uncoiled and part-severed, rendering the rest of it forever useless. She must have some kind of character flaw somewhere.

'Sorry to interrupt you both,' she says, gesturing to the small bottle in her hands. 'Liam's due his eye drops.'

I move out of her way and stand at the end of the bed as she administers the drops.

'He's been very communicative this week,' she tells me, with her back still turned. 'With me and with the occupational therapist. We've noted everything down... it's all in the book. It's made his eyes a bit tired though.'

She turns and gives me a smile, but I notice that it doesn't quite reach her eyes. I realise her previous offering when she'd first entered the room had done the same. What does she know? What has Liam said?

'Great. Thank you.' I feel heat rise at the back of my neck.

'Give me a call if there's anything you want to talk about later.'

Is that a usual offer? Of course, it is – whenever Liam has 'written' anything substantial before, it's always been discussed afterwards, whether between me and the staff at the unit or with people from external services who come in to work with Liam.

But there's a chance that whatever has been 'said' this week may have already been discussed before my visit here today, and I have no idea yet what Liam might have revealed.

When she leaves, I go straight to the drawer where the notebooks and letter boards are kept. I quickly scan through the pages until I find dates starting earlier this week.

She needs to be stopped. She's planning revenge. I've told her I don't want this, but she's not listening. I'm scared of what she might do.

And then I notice something. After this, a page has been torn from the notebook: neatly, but not so well that it hasn't left signs of its presence.

I glance at the door. Kathleen. I'd known there was something off in the way she'd looked at me before she'd left the room. She's usually so friendly, but today she'd been different.

'What have you told them?' I ask, waving the notebook in front of him. 'What have you said?'

But of course, Liam can't tell me, and even if he was able to, I doubt he would. I have told him too much, naïvely believing that my secrets would stay with him. That they were safe with his silence.

But of course, Liam is no longer silent. Not in every sense of the word, at least.

I quickly scan through the other notebooks, but there is nothing dated within the past few months. I shove the notebook in my bag. The letter boards stare out at me from the open drawer, but there's no time for that now. If Kathleen has already seen anything that might incriminate me, she may have already called the police.

'What have you done, Liam? You might have ruined everything.'

I realise I may not have much time to waste. Where has Kathleen gone? To call the police and let them know I'm here? I've no idea how much Liam has told them, but if the torn-out page of the notebook is anything to go by, he's told them enough. I can't wait around here to chance being caught.

'I love you very much,' I tell him, as I pull on my coat and throw my bag over my shoulder. 'I don't think you realise how much. I'd do anything for you, Liam. All of this has been for you.'

I kiss him on the cheek, and I feel his disapproval as strongly as had he spoken the words. I want to stay to clear the air between us, but we don't have time to talk things through, not now.

I pull his bedroom door closed behind me and hurry for the staircase. Halfway down, I hear a voice call out to me.

'Did you come in a van today?' the woman asks. 'It's blocking access for the deliveries.'

I don't recognise her, and I'm thankful that she's not one of the regular staff. 'I'm so sorry,' I tell her. 'I didn't realise. I'm just heading out anyway, though… I'll just sign out first.'

I return to the little entrance area where the visitor sign-in book rests open, and I check the time on my phone without noting it down beside my name. Should the police come here, I don't want them to know what time I left. I use the code to let myself out of the front door; relatives who are regular visitors are given access to it, and it's changed weekly for security reasons.

At the front of the car park, a food delivery van stands blocking the exit. The driver is standing outside. 'Sorry,' I call to him, gesturing to the black van where I'm guessing he usually parks. 'Just leaving.'

He gives me a thumbs up and gets back into the van, reversing out so that I can get past. I crane my neck to listen for any movement from the back, but there's nothing. There's CCTV in the nursing unit's car park, so I pull out on to the main road and drive another few streets before pulling into a lane that runs between two end-of-terrace houses. I get out and go to the back of the van, waiting a moment for any sounds or signs of motion. When there's nothing, I pull open one of the doors, bracing myself in case she tries anything clever. But nothing happens. The little bitch is still unconscious on the van floor.

FORTY-TWO

We are kissing. His lips are soft and taste like vodka, and his hands are in my hair. Above the music and the laughter that rings around the deck, I turn to whisper in his ear, suggesting we go somewhere quieter. He takes me by the hand and leads me inside the boat, where a flight of stairs close to the bar leads downstairs to a seating area with soft lighting and cushioned sofas.

He tells me his name is Liam. I like his accent, slightly northern and lilted, and when he says my name, he makes it sound like a question. We talk for a bit. He tells me he's on the island working for the summer, but when I ask what job he's doing here, he changes the subject. I don't mind not talking. The music is still loud, even from down here, and the cocktails are warming my blood. Life feels better in this moment than it has in a long time.

Then the boat seems to shift and sway, though it can't be real: the sea is still. It is beautiful outside, that pink-sky time between sunset and night. For the last three nights, Connor and I have sat and watched the sunset, mesmerised by the beauty and tranquillity of the place, despite its party reputation.

I tell him my name is Daisy. And then there is an explosion.

I am thrown sideways into Liam as the boat tilts wildly against the guttural boom that splits the air. My head hits something, dizzying me. He reaches for my hand, and I take it. He pulls me up, just as the deck above us collapses in on itself, crashing around us in a cloud of beams and metal, dust and glass. The boat's alarm goes off, ear-shattering and frantic.

A bright orange ball engulfs the upper deck, momentarily turning the sky into a haze of blinding white light. Dance music still pulses from the speakers, as though the party remains in full swing. As though the boat isn't filling with water. As though the two of us aren't stuck here, trapped, the water surging onboard as out on the deck people scream and panic and try to scrabble for a temporary safety.

I reach for his hand and squeeze his fingers between mine, silently praying to a god I'm cynical about at best, promising I will do better, if I can only be given a chance to.

I hear his voice in my dream as it came to me then: distant beyond the noise. 'My leg. I can't move my leg.'

I am faced with a choice: to leave him, or to try to save myself.

The water is rising around us. We are going to drown.

I am looking at his face, staring right into his deep brown eyes. He is just inches from me, and yet I cannot get to him to free him. My hands claw at the broken parts of boat that surround us, struggling with the beam that lies across the lower half of his body, my fingertips bleeding as I claw at the rough wood and steel. The dance music that was still blasting from the speakers just minutes ago has finally died. In its place is a tide of panicked screaming and the rush of water as it fills the lower deck of the boat.

'It's going to be okay,' I hear myself say, but my heart thunders with the lie.

The water is up to his chest now. It was slow at first, seeping gradually through his shorts, but now he is sitting in a pool, and it continues to rise as I lie to him. Behind me, there's a gap in the fallen structure that was once the floor of the top deck. I'm pretty sure I could make it through the space, just about. But it would mean leaving him behind. I couldn't live with myself... could I?

Overhead, the lighting flickers blue and white before we are plunged into darkness. I scream as a shower of sparks rains over us, sizzling as it hits the water. It is rising faster now, and black flumes of smoke pool the air like oil swirled on water. Where is Connor? He's a strong swimmer... I'm confident he'll be okay. But he has no idea where I am, and I know he'll come looking for me. The screams are floating away... the others are being rescued, safer in the ocean than they are inside this shell of a so-called party cruise. Liam is trapped, but I am not, and an escape lies just behind me, but I don't know what to do and we are both going to drown here.

'Daisy!'

I turn at my brother's voice. Through the fallen debris and the smoke that drifts in plumes from the engine room, I see Connor's silhouette wading through the knee-deep water. He has come to rescue me.

'I can't leave him!' I call above the noise.

'Who?'

He can't see him, I think. Down here, trapped in the inky darkness of a sea that is threatening to swallow us, Liam is already invisible.

'His name's Liam. His leg's trapped – one of the metal beams is pinning him down.'

There is an awful moment of silence that seems to stretch into forever. From a distance, the noise of emergency sirens begins to rise against the screaming and the splashing and the ominous creaking above our heads, the ship's structure groaning as more of it threatens to give way. Down here, just the three of us, we seem stuck within a timelessness I know will be broken once a decision is made. A devastating, life-altering choice that we will one way or another never be able to escape from.

It is Connor who breaks it.

'I'll come back for him,' he shouts to me. 'Just come on! We're running out of time.'

My fingers are still laced in Liam's, both of us shaking with the coldness of the water. The beautiful warmth of the Mediterranean sea has turned traitor on us, chilling us to our bones. I don't want to let go of his hand, but I know I must. As my fingertips slip from his, he calls out my name, his voice weakened by the pain of his crushed leg.

'We're coming back for you,' I tell him. 'We'll get help... I promise.'

I see the anguish in his eyes, the water rising further up his chest, and I turn away. The sound of sirens has risen to a scream. Help is here. Through the debris of the ship's carcass, Connor grabs for my hand and hauls me through the web of the wreckage. In his eyes, I see terror and determination. I fall into him, cut and bruised, and my brother pushes me towards the staircase.

'Go! I'll be right behind you.'

I watch as Connor tries to return to Liam, taking the makeshift path through which I've just left him, but as he does, the ship gives a yawning, guttural groan and the remaining section of ceiling collapses in front of him, blocking his route. I scream at Connor to come back, and when he turns to me, I see an expression I already know I'll never be able to erase from my memory.

Through the darkness and the wreckage, I try to see where Liam still lies, pinned to the floor of the boat. But I can't see anything. He is submerged now.

We're coming back for you... I promise.

It took me until that day – twenty-six years into my life, and already with so much trauma behind me – to learn that you should never make a promise you have no certainty of being able to keep.

FORTY-THREE

I wake with a loud gasp, and a pain in my chest so tight it feels as though I'm unable to breathe. I try to sit up, but I can't. My body is pinned to the floor, weighted by an invisible force. As my eyes struggle to gain focus on the shapes around me, I see bright white surrounding me. I'm not on the floor. I'm somewhere else... somewhere unfamiliar. My head... God, my head hurts so much. I was hit with something... I remember now.

There's a ringing in my ears. For a while there had been a crescendo of screams, a wail of alarms; the rushing, gushing surge of water. It was as alive and real as I was, and I was right back there, reliving every excruciating, drawn-out moment. Now, the sounds stay with me, ringing in my head, an audible nightmare.

I am staring at a ceiling. I can't do anything other than stare at the ceiling because I can't move my neck. I can blink, but I don't seem able to move anything else from the neck down, and even trying to turn my head requires an energy I don't have. When I try to, the pain in my brain surges like a flame pressed against my skull.

The ceiling isn't one I recognise. It isn't my home... I no

longer have a home. I don't think I'm at Andrew's house either... The ceilings are all smoothly plastered there, and white as white, freshly decorated. This is different. This is an older house, the ceiling cracked in places, the yellowing of age tinting the paintwork.

As my eyes begin to take focus, I see a mirror above a sink. There are toothbrushes in a cup holder, a tube of some kind of cream on the small shelf below the mirror. I realise now that I'm lying in a bath. I am cold... so cold that my fingers feel numb, although that could be the effects of whatever I've been given, because there's no doubt that I have been given something. I am paralysed here, trapped inside my own body.

I try to move my toes, but I can't. When I attempt to lift my right leg, it remains weighted to the bathtub. I concentrate on that area of my body, willing all my energy towards it, but nothing happens. Frustration and panic rise in my chest like a flood. I've no way of getting out of here, not without someone's help. But no one knows I'm here. I never saw Aisha's nana before I was struck across the head.

Just think... it won't be long before you get to see your brother again.

The last thing I heard before I fell unconscious. It was her voice. Rachel.

She must have found out about Connor online. I'd never told either of them about my brother. I'd never even told them his name. Yet I'd sensed soon after meeting her that she knew more about me than she was letting on, and now I know that my suspicions of her hatred for me were justified. Everything has been leading to this. There was a reason she kept questioning me, waiting for me to crack.

Past the screaming headache that rages at my temples and pulses in circuits around my skull, I picture that bag I found in her bedroom. My bag, stolen from me on the night I was attacked. Andrew. It wasn't him... I know it wasn't. But that doesn't mean he hadn't had some kind of involvement.

Everything has been a lie... all of it.

I try to open my mouth to call out, but my lips barely part, and not a sound escapes me. I wonder whether he knows that she has brought me here, wherever *here* is.

My arms are pinned at my sides; I might as well be tied down. I try to calm my thoughts by counting backwards from twenty, but by the time I get to one, my anxiety has skyrocketed. I try to console myself with thoughts that at least I know that Aisha is safe, but then I realise I don't know this at all. All I know is where she is. I still have no idea *how* she is. The woman from the hospital who I'd spoken to earlier had seemed to urge me to get there as quickly as possible, and why would she do that if Aisha was stable? More likely, she needed someone to reach her before it was too late.

A sob catches in my throat, but remains there, trapped and silent.

Her nana has no idea where Aisha is. I should have told her in that answerphone message which hospital she was at, because at least then, when I hadn't turned up to get her, Parveen would have known where to go. Now, Aisha is alone.

But the police are now looking for her, I tell myself. They will find her. They will contact Parveen. But then I remind myself just how apathetic the desk sergeant I'd spoken to had seemed. More likely, I'm on my own, and no one is looking for Aisha.

From behind me comes the creak of a door being opened. There are footsteps, slow and deliberate on what sounds like tiled flooring.

'Oh, good,' I hear Rachel say, her tone unmistakable. 'You're awake.'

She comes into view, blocking the light as she looms over

me. Her eye make-up is smudged. It looks as though she's been crying.

'Daisy,' she says, taking a seat on what I presume must be the closed toilet lid. 'I'm glad you've finally come round. We need to have a chat about my son. You remember him, don't you? Liam. I don't think you made it past first names in the way of introductions. Let me refresh your memory… he's the one you left to drown.'

FORTY-FOUR

I would do anything for my son.

The words she spoke to me weeks ago ring with a different sound now. This was never about Andrew. Andrew is her husband. Was he used as bait to lure me? I was naïve enough to fall into every trap they set for me. He knew exactly what he was doing, and I was stupid enough to believe he loved me.

'Surprise,' she says flatly. 'Had you forgotten about him?'

No, I hadn't, but my mouth won't move to tell her so. A weak groan escapes me.

'I'll take that as a yes. What's the matter, Daisy? Feel unpleasant to be trapped inside your own body? I'm guessing you'd found out what happened to Liam? You and your brother?'

Minutes after Connor had pulled me through the wreckage inside the boat, emergency crew rescued Liam from the water. He was airlifted to a hospital in Majorca, where Connor and I had gone to visit him. We hadn't been allowed to see him. I had never seen Rachel there. I would have remembered her. Had I met her, and had she looked me in the eyes and asked me what had happened, I would have told her everything. My brother had gone back for Liam, but he couldn't get to him.

'He was left alone to drown. You were the last person to speak to him. I think about that quite a lot. A stranger. You'd never known him before that day, and yet those last moments with him were gifted to you. And you left him to die.'

I had no idea until afterwards how long Liam had been submerged beneath the water by the time the emergency crew were able to release his leg. No one had thought he would make it, and I know Connor had assumed the worst and thought him already dead. The guilt and self-loathing had started in that moment, and it had never ended. When we'd got back to the UK, my brother had obsessed over Liam, trying to track his recovery, stalking his family members online in a search for updates on his condition. He went to therapy for a while, but nothing he was told could ease his sense of responsibility. He was haunted by the accident, plagued by PTSD. Within a little over a year later, my brother ended his own life.

'It took me quite a while to find you, Daisy. But it was worth the wait.'

This isn't going to change anything. I want to scream it at her, make her hear the words, that harming me won't bring back Connor and it won't change what happened to her son. It was an accident. There was no one to blame, other than whoever was responsible for ensuring that boat was safe to be out on the water. There was an inquiry into what had happened. A mechanical fault in the engine had caused the explosion, but no charges were brought against anyone.

She moves from the toilet and comes to the side of the bath, where she crouches down so that now all I see is her head at the side of the bathtub. 'Actually,' she says, resting her chin on her arms, 'I should be thanking you. For this past year, you've given me something to focus on. Do you know what it was like, getting that call? Having to fly to Spain knowing that when I got there, I'd find my only child in a coma? You can't even begin to imagine what a living hell I've been through. But you've offered me somewhere to channel all my anger. It should never have happened to Liam... he never deserved it.'

When Rachel moves from my side and goes to the far end of the bath, I see before it happens just what her terrifying plot for revenge entails. And I am completely helpless to stop it from unfolding.

'I can see why Andrew jumped at the opportunity I presented him,' she says, reaching for the plug. 'He likes them younger. Young and vulnerable... what does that say about him?' She leans into the bath and pushes the plug into the hole between my lifeless feet. Inside, I am screaming, but Rachel doesn't hear a sound. I try again to move my arms, my feet, to kick at her, to do something... anything. But nothing comes.

'Oh, you didn't think you were the only one, did you? Seven years we've been together. But he got the itch within less than two. Just before Liam—'

She cuts herself short, her face darkening at the memory of her husband's apparent infidelity. She seems angrier about this than she does about Liam.

And then she turns on the cold tap.

'Dead mother, dead father, dead brother. You seem to attract bad luck like shit attracts flies.'

I see myself flailing, struggling, fighting back. I hear myself crying, screaming, begging. Yet I see nothing other than Rachel, her face framed against the ceiling as I stare helplessly up at her, and I hear nothing other than the sound of water gathering beneath my legs. I am frozen, stuck here. Trapped. She takes one last look at my face, and then she leaves the room.

The perfect revenge.

The screams and the sirens come back to me as the bathroom morphs into a shipwreck. My eyes flit to my arms... my hands... and I see Liam's hand in mine, my fingers slipping from his as I let him go.

The water is an inch deep in the bath now, soaking through my clothes. It is cold and heavy, pinning me to the bottom of the tub. I close my eyes and picture Connor as he'd been on those first few days of that holiday: young, and for the first time in as long as I was able to remember, happy.

And my heart aches with the pain of missing him.

If I can just get my leg up to the tap, I'll be able to use my toes to turn it off. Even if I'm unable to turn it off completely, I'll at least be able to slow the flow. If I can just buy myself a little more time, I can try to think. I just need to think.

But I can't move either of my legs, and the water is rising. I lie here helplessly, haunted by the horror of the accident, reliving every terrifying moment as the bath fills around me. My knees disappear... my arms... my stomach. I watch as, bit by bit, by body is sucked beneath the water. It licks at my face before swallowing it. I am submerged, and I'm going to die here.

FORTY-FIVE

The first thing I feel is hands beneath my arms. They lift me in one sharp movement, sending water slopping from the rim of the bathtub across the tiled floor.

'Jesus Christ... what has she done to you?'

Andrew's voice. But I can't respond. A muffled groan escapes my lips as he lies me down on the bathroom floor.

'Daisy! Daisy, can you hear me?'

I feel fingers in my hair, assessing the injury she inflicted upon me at the hospital.

'Ummfh.'

'Shit.'

He pulls me half across his lap and rests his arm behind my head.

'Hello?' I hear him say. 'Yes... ambulance.' He reels off an address I'm unfamiliar with. I don't even recognise the name of the town. Where the hell am I? Is this their home? Their *real* home?

'Drowning. I mean... I don't know how long she's been in the water. Okay... okay...'

When I try to open my eyes, everything is blurred. I see the shape of Andrew, his head to the side with his phone balanced between his chin and shoulder. The room tilts as he moves me on to my side, presumably as instructed by the call handler.

'She isn't moving,' he tells the person at the other end of the call. 'She's floppy... I think she might have been drugged.'

The room comes in and out of focus, but as it does, I realise I'm able to move my fingers.

'Wait, she's trying to say something,' he says into the phone. 'Come quickly, please.'

I feel both his hands on me as he moves me on to the floor. Then he gets up and returns with a towel, putting it over me to try to keep me warm. He is kneeling above me now, telling me everything's going to be okay, saying sorry over and over to the point that I wish I could tell him to just shut the hell up. Because no number of apologies could undo what has happened. His wife was prepared to kill me. At some point, he was prepared to help her.

'Daisy, I am so sorry. I didn't know she'd go this far. I don't know what she's told you, but don't believe a word she says. This hasn't been for Liam. She was never any kind of mother to him. I'd known her for six months before she even mentioned that she had a son. They'd been estranged for years... Liam couldn't stand her. I only met him a couple of times, but he told me she was never there for him when he was growing up. She'd abandoned him by the age of ten... he was brought up by his grandmother. Everything she's done to you... this isn't for him. It's for her. She's trying to ease her own guilt.'

Stop talking. Stop talking, please.

But he doesn't hear me, and he keeps on going.

'All the things I told you about Rachel's mother... the drugs, the neglect, the terrible relationship. That was her and Liam. I married her before I knew who she was. I'm not expecting you to forgive me or to understand. I should never have gone along with what she planned. But then I let it start, and once it had, I didn't know how to back out of it. Things spiralled so quickly. And I liked you, Daisy. You've made me feel more normal than I've felt in a long time. I know I betrayed your trust... I let you down. I had to let Rachel think that everything between her and me was like it was before. That's why you saw us together, and I'm so, so sorry. I was trying to figure out a way of us getting to be together, with Rachel out of the picture. The more time you and I spent together, the more complicated everything became. I don't deserve your forgiveness but just listen to this, please, even if you don't want to hear anything else. I wish I had never done what I did. More than anything. I'm so sorry.'

I wonder how much of this one-sided conversation is being picked up by his phone, because as far as I'm aware, the 999 call was never ended. I can't think straight, but I'm able to think enough. Too much. The mugging outside work... the 'chance' meeting on the train. Oh my God... the burst pipe at the flat. Was that orchestrated to make the place uninhabitable, so that he could come to my 'rescue' by offering me a place to stay? The accusation at work... the stolen necklace planted in the handbag. All to alienate me and make me vulnerable. Make me dependent.

The past couple of months come crashing over me like a landslide.

'How beautifully touching. Quite a declaration of love.'

Rachel's voice hits me through the fog of Andrew's pathetic apology. He moves quickly, pushing himself up on to his feet.

'What have you done to her?'

'Nothing that she didn't do to my son.'

'This has gone too far,' Andrew says. 'You were never supposed to hurt her. You said you wanted her to understand what had happened to Liam.'

'And so she shall,' Rachel says, her words as sharp as blades of ice.

I try to turn my head. It moves slightly, the feeling starting to return to my bones as whatever Rachel gave me begins to weaken.

He shouts after her, but she leaves the bathroom and pulls the door closed behind her. I hear a key in the lock, then Andrew banging on the bathroom door, yelling at her to open it.

'Fuck. Fuck!'

He kicks something I can't see. *There's an ambulance on its way*, I want to tell him. He gave them the address. There's at least someone who knows that we're here.

'Rachel!'

And then he remembers the call. He looks around for his phone, finding it where he left it on the side of the sink. 'Hello? We've been locked in. We're in the bathroom on the first floor.'

I don't recognise the man standing just a couple of feet away from me. He wears the same clothes, he has the same face, but he is not the same person. A wave of memories washes over me: the concerned stranger on the train, the handsome face on our first date; the shoulder to cry on when I'd been suspended from work. I'm no longer sure whether the true evil is somewhere outside this room or if, in fact, I'm locked in with it. Rachel might have concocted this whole revenge plot, but Andrew has played out its starring role. And what a stellar performance he has delivered.

Andrew has stopped talking. He holds the phone away from his face and steps closer to the door, having heard something that my muted senses have apparently missed. I wiggle my fingers and then learn that I'm now able to do the same with my toes.

And then I hear it. A whoosh, like something surging upwards.

Like the searing, insidious lick of flames.

FORTY-SIX

It doesn't take long before we're able to smell the smoke. Andrew desperately tries the door handle, yanking it up and down until it seems it might snap off in his grip.

'Towels,' I manage to say.

He looks at me, taking a moment to understand what I'm instructing him to do. When he realises what I mean, he goes to the cupboard from where he'd got a towel for me earlier, grabs a handful and begins piling them against the bottom of the door, blocking the fumes from coming in through the gaps. Then he goes to the window and pushes the small square of glass open.

When he returns to his phone, he tells the 999 operator that a fire has been started.

'Hello? Hello? Shit! I've lost her.' He throws the phone into the sink. 'Are you able to move yet? Do you think you can sit up?' He comes over to me and helps me into an upright sitting position, pulling me towards the bathtub so that I'm able to lean against it.

'Why?' I manage to say, in a weak gasp. 'Why did you...'

Andrew sits on the tiles beside me. I hate him being this

close, but there's nothing I can do to get him away. It's taking all my energy just to stay upright.

'She wanted answers about what happened on that boat… about what happened to Liam. She made it all seem… I don't know. Justified. She talked about you so much… you and your brother became an obsession. She kept saying that she just wanted to talk to you, to get to know you, because you were a last link to the son she'd lost. I should have known that would never be enough for her. When she suggested I start a relationship with you, I thought at first that it was some kind of sick joke. But the more she spoke about it, the harder it became to deter her. I allowed myself to get swept along. There were things she threatened me with… infidelities that would have jeopardised my job. I let her blackmail me… I was weak. And then I met you, and everything spiralled.'

Everything spiralled. Like this has all somehow been my fault.

In truth, I think Andrew has derived some kind of sick pleasure from duping me into a fake relationship. This has been nothing more than a game to him. How entertaining it must have been for them, to watch my life unravel within their plans.

And now, with the fire surging from what sounds like not far beyond the bathroom door, I wonder whether they've despised each other for all this time as much as they've hated me.

'I never thought she'd harm you. She promised me that wasn't what she wanted… that this wasn't about revenge.'

'Bullshit.'

I feel relief that although I've not been able to say much to him, I'm at least able to expel this from my paralysed body. Everything he's told me is a lie. Our entire relationship has been constructed upon a desire for revenge.

Andrew gets up to retrieve his phone from the sink and then calls 999 again. He repeats the address to the call handler before being told there's help already on its way. He yanks at the handle again, then resorts to shoulder-barging the door, swearing at it as though expletives might be the added extra that was needed to force it to yield.

As the sensation in my fingers returns, I find myself now able to move my hands. I spread them flat on the floor at my sides, but my arms don't have the strength to straighten myself. Beyond the bathroom door, a succession of crackling, popping sounds confirms that wherever the fire has been started, it is edging closer.

'I don't love Rachel,' Andrew says, returning to the floor next to me. 'I haven't for a long time. I married her before I knew who she really was. I haven't been a good husband... she's probably already told you that. I wanted out, but I owed her. I don't know... I thought that maybe if I did this to help her, she'd make things easier for me when it came to a divorce. Stupid, I know. I already knew she hated me. But not like this... I never thought she'd be prepared to kill me.'

As though the thought of Rachel's betrayal has reignited his anger, Andrew gets back up and starts banging on the bathroom door again, yelling her name. But it's a waste of energy. Rachel is long gone. Outside the bathroom, there's a burst of noise as a window smashes against the force of the blaze. I can't cry... I can't panic. I feel numb and strangely calm.

Andrew turns and leans against the door, defeated. He looks at me, meeting my gaze, which must still appear vacant and glazed, here but not.

'I am so fucking sorry, Daisy. I'm sorry I lied... I'm sorry I deceived you. But not everything was fake. When I told you I loved you, that was real.'

I don't want my final moments to be spent listening to this, wasted on a man who never deserved my time or affection – someone who lied and manipulated, destroying my life so that he could then appear to be helping me rebuild it. He continues talking, taking advantage of the fact that I'm unable to respond, but I stop hearing anything he's saying. In my head, I'm sitting on a beach with my brother, the soft sand warming the backs of our legs as the shore gently ebbs and fades at our feet. That first day in Ibiza, in that precious snapshot of time between our lives' tragedies. I feel the sun on my face... the weightlessness of having nowhere to be and nothing to do. And for a moment, I might almost believe myself back there.

Help isn't coming. As the fire surges outside, smoke starts to fill the room, billowing in clouds through the gaps around the door, despite Andrew's attempts to block its course. I'm already feeling lightheaded again... woozy... and I know it's not just from whatever Rachel drugged me with. Andrew and I are both going to die here. Rachel might not have got the ending she'd planned for me, but she's achieved my demise all the same.

He moves to the window and gulps greedily at the small square of fresh air. The space is too small for us to get through, and how would he get me up and out of here anyway, my body still limp and as good as lifeless? But perhaps that's just it. Maybe he doesn't mean to take me with him. Despite my earlier sense of calm, the thought of being left alone here terrifies me.

'Please,' I manage to say, 'don't... don't leave me here.'

There is a dull thud from somewhere out on the landing. There is shouting and banging, and as the door bursts open and a fireball rips through the room, Andrew throws himself at me, using his body to cover mine.

FORTY-SEVEN

The service is short and solemn. I stay at the back, keeping a respectful distance from the family and other mourners, who I still feel I have no right to stand among. It is strange that death unites people in such a way. I wonder how many people in this room are familiar with one other beyond the shared experience of having known the deceased. Many may never have crossed paths before, and yet all have either loved or respected or looked up to this man at some moment in their lives, enough to want to be here today to pay their last respects.

It was raining on the day of Connor's funeral. Everyone had worn something blue, as a nod to the football team my brother had followed since a child. I hadn't expected many to attend; he hadn't stayed in touch with his school friends, and he hadn't been in any job for longer than a year – not long enough to forge the kind of relationships that stick and stay. Yet on the morning of the funeral, the street on which the church stood was lined with people wearing blue, and the church was so full that former colleagues and acquaintances waited in the church doorway and out in the graveyard.

I had moved through the motions that day, at once appreciative for the efforts that people had made, while resentful of their absence when it had been most needed. Where had these people been when Connor was ravaged with nightmares about that night? Who had parted with kind words and made offers of support when he was plagued with the guilt that had eventually killed him? My expectations were unreasonable, and my bitterness was unfair. We are all just trying to navigate our own paths through this life, all desperately finding a way to stay afloat.

Yousuf's photograph rests on an easel at the front of the room. A prayer is spoken by the imam, and when the rest of the people in the room lower their heads, I do the same. If it's forgiveness we're all asking for, I may need it more than anyone.

With my head still lowered, my eyes dart nearer to the front of the mosque, where Aisha stands with Parveen, their hands held. We haven't had a chance to speak yet today. I asked for her permission to be here, and she granted it, and for that I am grateful. It's more than I deserve.

Yousuf died a week after being admitted to hospital. He'd remained in the ICU after his stroke, but just twenty-four hours after being moved to a ward he suffered a massive heart attack. Aisha was still in hospital recovering from the assault when he passed away. She had been struck across the head after leaving work and had been found on the banking by the River Taff by a young couple who were walking home after a night out in the city. Witness statements, along with CCTV close to Cardiff castle, helped confirm Rachel as Aisha's attacker. She'd become desperate and careless, and Aisha was a potential threat. By telling her too much about my suspicions surrounding Rachel, I had inadvertently made Aisha a second target.

When the service ends, the mourners at the back of the room begin to filter outside, to the cemetery at the back of the building. I go with them and wait as an orderly queue is formed, people offering their condolences one by one as Parveen and Aisha make their way outside. Despite having been to see her in hospital, and having already visited Parveen's home since Yousuf's death, I can't bear to face them. I still feel responsible for so much of what has happened.

'I'm sorry,' I say, as Parveen reaches for my hand. Her fingers feel cold in mine, and though she says nothing in response, I know that her touch alone signals her forgiveness. She moves to the person standing next to me, and then I find myself face to face with Aisha.

'I never got to say goodbye,' she says, so quietly that her words are almost a whisper. I'm not sure whether it's appropriate to do so, but I reach for her and pull her towards me, grateful when she rests her face on my shoulder and cries there silently, letting me hold her.

'Aisha. I'm so, so sorry.'

I feel her body tense against mine, and I know she understands. I am sorry she has lost her beloved grandfather, but there is also so much more I need to apologise for. I'm not sure whether she'll ever be able to forgive me for everything that has happened and everything I unwittingly dragged her into, but I hope that in time she might.

'I'm sorry too,' she says quietly. 'I'm sorry I doubted you.'

She stands back, quickly composing herself in front of her relatives and family friends. Her hair hides the scar that was left when Rachel attacked her that Friday night as she made her way home on foot, and the fractured cheekbone she sustained when she'd hit the ground has thankfully healed without leaving a mark. But I know the psychological wounds will take far longer to recover from.

I put a hand to my cheek, my fingers running a path where my own scar lies, a souvenir from the evening I was mugged.

'Later?' she says, the word lilted as a question.

I nod. I'll wait for as long as she needs me to.

I walk with the other mourners as they make their way to the cemetery, where Yousuf's coffin is waiting to be lowered into the ground. Aisha and Parveen remain stoic as they observe the ritual, and when they both step forward to scatter soil on to the coffin, I look away, feeling as though I'm intruding on a moment that is too private and personal to be shared.

Later, I return to the Travelodge that has been my home for the past ten days. During that time, there have been countless police interviews and statements given, samples taken and evidence provided. I have been asked the same questions over and over, as though the police have at some point expected my version of events to suddenly change. But the truth doesn't alter, and an honest tongue doesn't need to rely on memory.

Rachel and Andrew are both in custody. The house she'd taken me to had been their marital home in a suburb of Bristol, where they'd lived for the past six years. After Andrew and I had been pulled from that bathroom, the building had burned nearly to the ground.

I'm lying on the bed, alone with my thoughts when the phone rings. It's Aisha.

'What are you doing tomorrow?' she asks me.

I hadn't given it a thought. I'd forgotten that tomorrow is Christmas Day.

'Nothing.'

'I thought, if it's okay with you, we could go to visit Connor together?'

I bite my bottom lip to stop myself from crying. Every Christmas since he died, I've gone to Connor's graveside to sit and talk to him. I tell him about work and what I've been up to, sharing the details I know he would want to hear. I tell him how much I miss him. How much I would part with for just another couple of minutes with him.

Sometimes, I believe that he's somehow able to hear me.

With no public transport running on Christmas Day, for the past three years it's been Aisha who's driven me there. I never would have thought she would make the same offer now.

'Are you sure?'

'It's tradition, isn't it?'

And with those four simple words, I know I'm forgiven.

FORTY-EIGHT

The member of staff who greets me at the front door has a badge pinned to her chest with the name Kathleen. She asks me to sign in the visitor's book before she taps a code to let us into the main building. She is chatty and animated, and I wonder how she retains so much joy and positivity when surrounded by so much suffering. I suppose this is exactly the kind of person suited to this role.

'You understand the nature of his condition?' she asks, as she leads me to Liam's bedroom. 'Liam is aware of everything that's going on around him. There's no issue with his mental capacities. Whatever you say to him it will be heard and understood.'

I nod.

'He's communicated something for you,' she says. 'It's waiting in his room. Perhaps you should read it first, before you see him?'

I wait in the corridor as she goes to Liam's room, where I hear her greet him cheerfully, asking him if he's comfortable. She comments on the glorious day outside, and it is – a beautiful mid-March afternoon, warmer than average for the time of year.

She asks if he'd like her to open the window, and I know from what I've already learned of Liam that he'll be using eye blinks to respond to the offer.

When she returns, she has a typed letter in her hand. 'Take your time, love,' she says, handing it to me. 'There's a day room just along the corridor... there's no one in there at the moment. Perhaps you'd be better reading it there?'

She shows me to the room before leaving me alone to read the letter.

Dear Daisy,

Hello again. I'd hoped after we'd met that I might see you again after that day, though I could never have guessed it would be like this. Don't leave it so long next time, haha! There are a few things I need you to know. Firstly, I don't blame you for what happened that day. I don't blame your brother, either. The explosion was an accident, and there was no one to blame. I know you couldn't free my leg, and I know that Connor came back for me. I remember him being there. His desperation. I heard about what happened to him, and I'm sorry. If I'd ever had a chance to speak to him, I would have told him that I never blamed him.

The second thing I need you to know is that I had nothing to do with my mother's plans. I never gave her your name, or Connor's. I never wanted revenge, and she never explicitly told me about her intentions towards you. But she started to say things that made me suspicious, and I grew worried that she might hurt someone. I'm so sorry it was you. She never really bothered with me much when I was a kid, and I'd always wondered why she was so ambivalent towards me when I was growing up. But after the accident, I couldn't get rid of her. Careful what you wish for, eh?!

I have good days and bad days. On the bad days, I hate the world and everyone in it. I wonder why me, and I torture myself by going through all the bad things I might have done when I was younger that may have been the reason why I was punished this way. But on others, I realise I didn't do anything. It was just bad luck... chance... whatever. Wrong place, wrong time. I can still listen to music and watch the sun set beyond the trees outside my window (not quite like the Ibiza sunsets, but still pretty special in their own way). I can still watch the football. Maybe one day I'll be able to eat ice-cream again. In the meantime, I've still got the memory of it. It's the little things I miss the most. The smell of rain... walking the dog... giving someone a hug. But I can communicate now, and that makes everything easier. Who knows... maybe one day I might write a book.

I'm still glad we met, despite the circumstances. In another life, who knows, perhaps we might have kept in touch. Enjoy your life, Daisy – it is precious.

Liam x

Without me knowing at which line of his letter it had started, I am crying. Fat tears streak my cheeks and there's a pain in my chest like a fist gripped around my heart. I read the letter four times, and each time I find something new within it.

'Here.' Kathleen has returned to the room and is standing beside me, holding out a box of tissues. 'Don't let him see you like this, eh?'

I nod and pull a tissue from the box, wiping my eyes as I try to catch my breath.

'Are you ready?'

I get up and follow her to Liam's room.

'Pull the cord if you need me for anything.'

When I go into the room, Liam is sitting with his head turned away from me, facing the window. I don't want to startle him, so I say his name before I move in front of him. I try not to appear shocked at how different his appearance is now to the young man I'd met on that party cruise five and a half years ago.

'Hey,' I say. 'Thank you for your letter. It's helped. It's really helped, actually... more than you know.'

There's a visitors' chair in the corner, which I pull into the middle of the room so that I can sit with him. 'She seems nice,' I say, gesturing to the door. I already don't know what to say. Does this get easier over time? I imagine it must. I was advised to keep talking, but now I'm here, my tongue seems to have seized up in my head, and I don't know what to say to him. I can't talk about his mother or what has happened... I can't talk about our only shared experience, which was the day of the accident. Everything feels tainted by tragedy and sadness.

I glance outside. It's early evening, and the sun is beginning to drop beyond the trees outside the window.

'I was wondering... if it's okay with you... I thought we could watch the sunset together. Would that be okay?'

I look at him and get a single blink – yes – and with a smile, I pull my chair closer to his and take his hand in mine.

EPILOGUE

Rachel doesn't look up as the jury re-enters the room. She sits by her defence lawyer with her head lowered, her blonde hair hanging against her face. He leans to her and whispers something in her ear, just as the judge calls for order in the courtroom. All attention moves to the foreman of the jury.

'On the first charge of attempted murder, we find the defendant...'

In the public gallery, Aisha's hand tightens around mine as I hold my breath.

'Guilty.'

I exhale like a deflated balloon.

'On the second charge of attempted murder, we find the defendant... guilty.'

Aisha is squeezing my hand so tightly she's probably cut off the circulation to my fingers. Rachel still hasn't raised her head. A series of other charges – abduction, GBH, perverting the course of justice – are given verdicts, but I stop hearing anything. My head and heart feel light with relief. Finally, after months of being cross-examined and interrogated... finally, this is all over.

Rachel receives a sentence of eighteen years. Andrew is already serving his three-year sentence – his trial having finished much earlier than Rachel's. The list of offences against him wasn't so lengthy, and the fact that he had saved my life helped towards a lessening of his sentence. He's written to me since being in prison, but I didn't read it. I burned the unopened envelope.

'Coffee?' Aisha suggests, as we leave the court building. I could do with something stronger, but as Aisha doesn't drink alcohol, caffeine will have to do.

We walk a few streets away from the court before finding a cafe. 'The usual?'

I find a table while Aisha orders us two caramel lattes and a slab of chocolate brownie so big it's enough for the two of us to share. The instant hit of caffeine and sugar tastes like heaven on my tongue.

'I'm sorry I put you through all this.'

'Listen, Miss White,' Aisha says, running a finger along her top lip to remove a small cloud of froth, 'I'll allow you to do this today, but can we please make a pact? After today, we move on. No more apologies. No more dwelling on the things we can't change. No more shoulda woulda coulda. Make a promise, please.'

'I promise.'

'Okay. So now, make the most of your final hours of rumination. Go.'

'I just keep going over everything,' I tell her, not wanting to draw this conversation out for longer than it deserves. We've already been around in circles with it all so many times over these past few months. 'And I keep coming back to why. Why did I fall for it? Why didn't I see what was going on?'

'Because it was exciting. Because your life has been so routine for so long that he offered something you didn't know you wanted... not until it was put in front of you. I don't think you've been living, Daisy... not in the true sense of the word. Since Connor died, it's like you've felt too guilty to live. Andrew made you feel alive. It wasn't your fault for welcoming the feeling.'

With just a few sentences, Aisha has managed to condense my experience more succinctly than any therapist has ever before achieved. I'm so grateful for it that I could cry, but my tears dried up a long time ago now.

'He already knew details of your life,' she continues. 'He knew how to manipulate you to get you close. He and Rachel had researched your background. It isn't your fault. You aren't weak, Daisy. You're a victim. They're not the same thing.'

Rachel had hired someone to attack me that evening after I had left the department store. It couldn't be proven, but of course Andrew must have known. How else would he have been there on that train, my knight in shining armour? There's no such thing as coincidence, not where Rachel's concerned, at least. During the investigation, other things came to light. By the time I went to stay at what I'd believed was Andrew's home – a house they had rented with the intention of luring me there – Rachel had been involved with another man for six months. She'd been planning to leave Andrew but had wanted to do so in a way that would have left her with the majority of their assets. She became too greedy, too wrapped up in her desire for revenge on Andrew and on me, and eventually the control she'd believed herself to have had started to unravel from her grip. She had attacked Aisha to silence her and had then taken her phone to text her nana. She'd gleaned enough from my conversations with Andrew to know that Aisha lived with her grandparents, and messaging Parveen delayed the inevitability of someone looking for Aisha.

Yet although Rachel was the mastermind behind her revenge plot, Andrew wasn't as innocent as he'd liked to make out either. He'd burst the pipe in my living room knowing exactly what he was doing and had sent me into the bathroom using the guise that I should 'relax' so that he could use a pipe-detecting device to locate exactly where he needed to drill to cause maximum damage. He'd known that Rachel had been into my flat with the key that had been taken in my bag on the evening I was mugged, and he knew that she'd installed a camera in my room, so tiny that I had missed it. He'd had sex with me in my bed to taunt her, knowing that she'd watch every second of it. The shoes that had been bought with Rachel's card on the day she'd pushed me down the stairs had been purchased by Andrew, though he continued to claim he'd had no idea what Rachel had been planning. The man might have pleaded some warped version of what he thought love might have looked like, but he was as guilty as his wife.

'Look,' Aisha says, reaching for her phone, 'you can talk to me as much as you want, you know that. We'll go over it all as many times as you need to. But there's something I need to show you. It's going to go quickly.'

She taps her phone screen before holding it up to me. It's a listing for a two-bed rental property on the outskirts of Cardiff.

'It's a terrace,' she says, 'and look.' She swipes across a few photographs. 'It's even got a little garden. What do you reckon?'

We've been talking about looking for a house or flat share for the past month or so. Since the new year, I've been renting a room from a divorcee who doesn't ask questions and rarely speaks to me much, which has suited me perfectly. But I'd like to get more space back, and now that I'm back at work, the money side of things should hopefully get easier.

'Let's book a viewing.'

'Really? Okay... this is brilliant. I'll call them now.'

I keep thinking about what Liam wrote in his letter to me. I'm going to see him again in a couple of weeks, and I'll keep visiting once a month for as long as he wants me to. I've still got his letter, kept inside a book in my bedside table. I've read it so many times that I'm able to recite it, word for word.

It's the little things I miss the most. The smell of rain... walking the dog... giving someone a hug.

'Come on,' Aisha says, pulling her jacket from the back of her chair. 'We'll have to get a taxi if we're going to make it in time.'

I realise that for the last minute or so, my brain had left the coffee shop.

'Did you hear me?' she asks, pulling her jacket up over her shoulders. 'They've got a viewing free in half an hour.' She looks to the front of the shop. 'Oh, great,' she says, gesturing to the rain that's now lashing against the front windows. 'You got an umbrella?'

'No,' I say, pulling on my coat. 'Don't worry about it... we won't shrink.'

When we get out on to the street, I put my arms around her and pull her in for a hug.

'What was that for?' she asks with a laugh. 'We haven't got the place yet.'

'Just... thank you. For everything.'

We wait for a gap in the traffic before crossing the road to the train station, where a row of taxis is always waiting outside.

'Aisha?' I say, raising my voice against the rain.

'Yeah?'

'How would you feel about getting a dog?'

A LETTER FROM VICTORIA

Dear Reader,

I'd like to say a massive thank you for choosing to read *It's Me or Her*. Every book purchase, library loan and recommendation to a friend is appreciated, and I feel blessed to still be doing my dream job. I loved writing this one – Rachel's character, in particular – and I hope you've enjoyed Daisy's journey. If so, and you would like to keep up to date with all my latest releases, just sign up at the following link. Your email will never be shared, and you can unsubscribe at any time.

www.bookouture.com/victoria-jenkins

I love reading revenge plots, and Rachel's mission for vengeance against Daisy might be one of the most twisted I've written. While writing the book, I did a lot of research on 'locked-in' syndrome – on the causes, the effects, and on individual cases of victims and their families. I read *The Diving Bell and the Butterfly* – the astonishing account of Jean Dominique-Bauby, who found himself 'locked-in' and unable to communicate after suffering a stroke. His determination to express himself – the book written using single eye-blinks – is a true testament to the endurance of the human spirit, and it is a highly recommended read.

I hope you loved reading *It's Me or Her* as much as I enjoyed writing it – and if so, I would be very grateful if you could write a review. I love to hear your thoughts, and they really do make a difference in helping new readers discover one of my books for the first time.

Thank you,

Victoria

        X x.com/vicwritescrime
        ⌾ instagram.com/vicwritescrime

ACKNOWLEDGEMENTS

Thank you to all the readers, new and old, who continue to read and enjoy my books – it means the world. Thank you to my editor, Laura Deacon, who does a brilliant job at pulling my ideas into shape and bringing the stories to life. Thank you also to her great team at Bookouture, and to all the marketing and publicity staff who put my stories out into the world. And thank you to my family – your support is everything.

PUBLISHING TEAM

Turning a manuscript into a book requires the efforts of many people. The publishing team at Bookouture would like to acknowledge everyone who contributed to this publication.

Audio
Alba Proko
Sinead O'Connor
Melissa Tran

Commercial
Lauren Morrissette
Hannah Richmond
Imogen Allport

Cover design
The Brewster Project

Data and analysis
Mark Alder
Mohamed Bussuri

Editorial
Laura Deacon
Melissa Tran

Copyeditor
Donna Hillyer

Proofreader
Liz Hatherell

Marketing
Alex Crow
Melanie Price
Occy Carr
Cíara Rosney
Martyna Młynarska

Operations and distribution
Marina Valles
Stephanie Straub
Joe Morris

Production
Hannah Snetsinger
Mandy Kullar
Nadia Michael
Charlotte Hegley

Publicity
Kim Nash
Noelle Holten
Jess Readett
Sarah Hardy

Rights and contracts
Peta Nightingale
Richard King
Saidah Graham

RAISING READERS
Books Build Bright Futures

Dear Reader,

We'd love your attention for one more page to tell you about the crisis in children's reading, and what we can all do.

Studies have shown that reading for fun is the **single biggest predictor of a child's future life chances** – more than family circumstance, parents' educational background or income. It improves academic results, mental health, wealth, communication skills, ambition and happiness.

The number of children reading for fun is in rapid decline. Young people have a lot of competition for their time, and a worryingly high number do not have a single book at home.

Hachette works extensively with schools, libraries and literacy charities, but here are some ways we can all raise more readers:

- Reading to children for just 10 minutes a day makes a difference
- Don't give up if children aren't regular readers – there will be books for them!

- Visit bookshops and libraries to get recommendations
- Encourage them to listen to audiobooks
- Support school libraries
- Give books as gifts

There's a lot more information about how to encourage children to read on our websites: **www.RaisingReaders.co.uk** and **www.JoinRaisingReaders.com**.

Thank you for reading.

Printed in Dunstable, United Kingdom